BETTY STEADY

AND THE QUEEN'S ORB

First published in Great Britain in 2025 by Farshore
An imprint of HarperCollins*Publishers*
1 London Bridge Street, London SE1 9GF

farshore.co.uk

HarperCollins*Publishers*
Macken House, 39/40 Mayor Street Upper, Dublin 1, D01 C9W8

ISBN 978 0 00 860037 2

Printed and bound in the UK using 100% renewable electricity at
CPI Group (UK) Ltd

1

A CIP catalogue record for this title is available from the British Library.

This book contains FSC™ certified paper and other controlled
sources to ensure responsible forest management.

For more information visit: www.harpercollins.co.uk/green

NICKY SMITH-DALE

ILLUSTRATED BY
SaRah HoRNE

BETTY STEADY

AND THE QUEEN'S ORB

Farshore

for Mum, Dad and Carly

CRAG OF INSTABILITY

TOXIC FOREST OF ETERNAL FIRE

Mount CRUMBLE DOWN

WOBBLY ROCK

NOT TODAY, THANK YOU!

N
N.N.N.N
N.N.N.N
EAST

W   E

S.S.S.S
S.S.S.S
WEST

S

THE GREAT LAKES OF PECKISH PILCHARD

HULLO.

GIANT MUSHROOM MAZE OF THE FUNGAL JUNGLE

Map of WOBBLY ROCK

Chapter 1

ello there, lovely reader. Thanks for choosing this book! You can give yourself three house points for having such good taste.

Now, if for some reason you've not heard of me, I'll introduce myself. I'm Salvador Catflap, the greatest storyteller in the distant and magical land of Wobbly Rock. (There is one other writer here, a farmer called Clammy Pete, but unfortunately he's lost confidence since his poem, *There Was a Young Bee Named Steve*, received disappointing reviews.)

Anyway, I thought you'd like to know that last Tuesday, I received a letter from a young lad named Dave Schoolboy, who lives over there in your 'normal world'. It said:

Dear Salvador Catflap,

I recently finished your first book about Betty Steady. What an adventure! I laughed so much, my nose fell off. I cried so hard, my hamster needed a lifeboat. Hands down, best story ever. Please, PLEASE write another instalment. I'll simply eat my own eyebrows if you don't.

Yours hopefully,

Dave Schoolboy

Well, who am I to deny my fans? A sequel you want? A sequel you will have. But first, there are a few things you need to know:

Betty Steady was an absolute champion. She was only twelve, but she was a **RIGHT TOUGH NUT**. Known as

the Guardian of Wobbly Rock, she defended her beloved castle from all kinds of baddies.

Thanks to a horrid shrinking spell - cast by a wicked Toad Witch - Betty was *tiny*. I mean tiny tiny. Like she couldn't even sniff your kneecaps on tiptoe.

And finally, reader, there a few poems scattered throughout this book. I promised Clammy Pete I'd showcase some of his new work. Poor old thing's been feeling a bit down on his luck lately. He'd love some feedback. Just a warning, though . . . the chap's obsessed with bees. I mean OBSESSED.

Right, I think we're ready. Get yourself a comfy cushion and a glass of pineapple squash and settle in for a bowlful of Betty.

In Betty Steady's bedroom, at the top of the castle of Wobbly Rock, the Crossword Crew were having another epic sleepover. Betty lay in her cosy bed, in the doll's house she'd borrowed from her best pals Pam and Pamm.

'What a **WILD** night,' she said, as jolly as a jelly baby.

Her friend Figg was sleeping beside a pile of word puzzles, wearing his trademark bumbag. Even though he was a right paperwork nerd, Betty had grown to love the little green imp. On the sofa next to him, Elle Emen-O'Pea the mouse was snoring under an empty packet of custard creams, clutching her little trumpet. And Rupert Sometimes, an utter gentleman of an owl, was tucked up with a book of cryptic crosswords rolled into a pillow, dreaming of his favourite thing in the world. (Bin day.)

Of course, the twin princesses of Wobbly Rock, Pam and Pamm, were there too, sucking each other's thumbs. Although they weren't *technically*

part of the Crossword Crew, they always loved to
join the gang for a good old knees-up. And blimey,
it had indeed been a good old knees-up, full of
crosswords, jazz solos from Elle Emen-O'Pea, and a
tense game of *pin the wig on the weasel.*

Watching them sleep, Betty felt a strange bubbly
feeling in her stomach. No, it wasn't gas. It was
love. These cool characters were the greatest chums
Betty could ever ask for! It was an honour to be

6

besties with such a bunch of **PARTY ANIMALS**.

Careful not to wake her friends, Betty climbed up the curtain and sat on the window ledge. Being so little (approximately the height of a can of spaghetti hoops), she could fit on the narrow window ledge with room to spare. She took a deep breath and admired the view from the castle, high on Mount Crumbledown. As the breeze blew through her big reddish-brown curly hair, the moon shone over the valley like a radiant pickled onion.

'No one defeats the Guardian of Wobbly Rock,' Betty whispered to herself, as her eyes grew heavy.

But, just as she was about to drift off to sleep, she heard a noise below. Out in the darkness, a figure on horseback was making its way towards the castle door.

Betty snapped awake. **'COME ON, GANG!'** She leaped from the window. **'CODE BROWN!'**

Figg woke up with a snort. 'Code Brown? Crikey. You grab some gloves while I find a long brush.'

'Brush?' said Betty. 'No . . . there's an intruder!'

Figg shook his head. 'How many times, Betty? You must learn the colour-code system. Code *Raspberry* is an intruder. Code *Brown* is for a blocked toilet chute.'

Betty flapped her tiny hands. 'Oh, twaddle cakes. Just hurry up.'

Pam and Pamm scurried off to inform their father of the emergency, clutching their crowns as they ran. (Pam's crown was a colourful garland of freshly cut flowers, while Pamm sported her usual crown of freshly cut bread.)

Rupert Sometimes shook out his feathers. 'Hop on, you beauts,' he said.

The Crossword Crew knew the drill. Everyone climbed on to Rupert Sometimes' strapping back and they took off into the darkness like a gang of fearless fondant fancies.

Readying herself for a fight, Betty came up with a plan. *Use the element of surprise. Use the help of her awesome pals. Use a pair of tweezers to pinch the intruder's snivelling nose.* **KNICK-KNACK, PADDY WHACK!**

Rupert Sometimes and the gang swooped down towards the stranger. He was a boy not much older than Betty, dressed in lacy pantaloons, a velvet tunic and a feathered hat.

Betty did a triple somersault and landed between the ears of the boy's horse. Then, like two clever ping-pong balls, Figg and Elle Emen-O'Pea

launched themselves from the bird, bounced off
each other and landed on the boy's shoulders.
Before he could react, they pulled back his ears so
his face resembled a lump of stretched pizza dough.

As the boy brought his horse to an abrupt stop,
Betty held the tweezers to his nose.

'**WHO ARE YOU, FANCY PANTS?**'
she demanded. '**AND WHAT DO YOU
WANT?**'

etty tugged at the boy's nostril hairs.

'I said, **WHO ARE YOU?!'**

'I'm Andy Underarm.' The boy

gulped. 'The . . . the queen's personal

messenger.'

'What queen?' asked Betty.

Andy Underarm loosened his collar. 'Queen

McNiff, miss. From the kingdom of Upper Crust.'

Shaking, he took a roll of parchment from his satchel.

'I'm here to deliver an invitation to King Nutmeg.'

'Invitation?' Betty snatched the parchment. 'If you're lying, *you'll* be getting an invitation . . . to a party with Linda and Gregg!'

'Sounds n-n-nice?' said Andy Underarm, unsure what kind of parties this Linda and Gregg were into.

Betty flexed her arms. **'LINDA AND GREGG ARE MY BICEPS, BUDDY. THEY DON'T DO NICE.'** Laughing, she began to untie the ribbon from the parchment.

'Betty, no!' cried Figg, letting go of the boy's ear. 'Opening the king's personal post? Just when I thought you were grasping basic royal etiquette. Do you need to see my PLOP again?'

'Your what?'

'My *Protocol, Law and Ordinance Presentation*,' said Figg.

'Ugh. No stinking way!' said Betty.

Elle Emen-O'Pea released her grip on the boy's other ear, which pinged forward and smacked him on the nose. 'Personally, I think we should let him inside. He seems honest enough.'

Betty scrunched up her face and looked the boy dead in the eyes. 'Well, I don't trust him. **HE AIN'T WELCOME ROUND HERE.'**

'P-please . . .' Andy Underarm spluttered. 'It's an invitation to the Turnip Festival.'

Betty's stomach set off a party popper. Her intestines began a conga line with all her other internal organs. Oh, how she'd always dreamed of attending Upper Crust's legendary Turnip Festival!

'The celebrations begin in four days,' Andy Underarm said. 'And all the king's best pals are invited to come too.'

'Whoops. Did I say you're **NOT** welcome round here?' Betty lowered her tweezers and let her face unscrunch. 'I meant to say **YOU'RE EXTREMELY WELCOME! GET YOURSELF INSIDE FOR A FIZZY POP RIGHT NOW!'**

News of the invitation spread quickly around

the castle. Reader, I'm sure you can understand the level of excitement. Imagine, for a moment, that *you* were invited to the greatest celebration of root vegetables known to mankind. You'd put on your party pants and sing *My Life is Brilliant* at the top of your voice, that's for sure.

I'm assuming you have similar festivities in your world? Some sort of Onion Carnival or Beetroot Gala? Naturally, you're familiar with the kind of entertainment you'd find there. Turnip Parade. Pass the Parsnip. Hide the Sprout. That sort of thing.

Believe me, the courtiers of Wobbly Rock were practically eating each other's belly-button fluff to get an invite.

When Figg handed King Nutmeg the invitation the next morning, the king's long face rose into a cheesy smile. 'Pickled pie crusts!' he said. 'The Turnip Festival? Don't mind if I do!'

'Daddy, can we come?' said Pam and Pamm, with pleading puppy-dog eyes.

14

'Of course you can, my splendid daughters,' said the king. 'Now, let's see . . . I'll also need my Royal Adviser, Figg. And my exquisite First Royal Trumpeter, Elle Emen-O'Pea.'

Betty peered up at the throne, expecting to hear her name called out at any moment. Andy Underarm stood awkwardly in the corner, hoping he might get a fizzy pop.

'And naturally we'll need Rupert Sometimes for transportation.' The king stroked his beard. 'Who else?'

'Well, obviously, I'm coming,' said Betty, as she scurried to safety, far from the king's tapping foot. 'As your personal bodyguard.'

The king looked her up and down. It didn't take long because she was so small. 'Hmmm,' he said. 'How do I put this?'

Betty scowled. **'HEY, I MAY BE SMALL, BUT I CAN BRAWL.'**

'Yes, Betty. I know you can fight,' said King Nutmeg. 'You've saved our bacon many a time. It's just . . .'

Betty put her hands on her hips. **JUST WHAT?**

'It's just that this trip is a chance to showcase the *strength* of Wobbly Rock,' said King Nutmeg. 'To let Queen McNiff and all those Upper Crust poshos know that we're just as powerful as them. And . . . well, while *we* know you're as tough as toffee, outsiders might see it as a weakness if my personal bodyguard is no taller than a cheese grater.'

'Wise decision, Your Highness,' said Figg. But when Betty shot him a dirty look, he backtracked. 'I mean . . . don't forget Betty *is* an asset, despite her puny stature.'

'No,' decided the king. 'My Royal Bodyguards will be Sir Loin of Beef, who will come out of retirement especially for the occasion, and Johnny Logflume, thanks to his recently rediscovered kung fu skills.'

'Drat,' muttered Betty, knowing full well that

Johnny Logflume, the Second Royal Flagbearer, was utterly fab at kung fu.

'But, of course, Great Guardian, you will be my tiny, secret security,' said the king. 'My undercover spy. My confidential commando. It's just that those strapping lads *look* the part. You do understand, don't you, little cupcake?'

'LITTLE CUPCAKE?!' Betty grimaced. 'I'm a ten-tier fruitcake with extra nuts. And anyway, who cares if I don't look the part when I've got the **SKILLS?'**

From the moment he'd first laid eyes on her dinky size, Betty had reminded King Nutmeg of his first pet, Tiddles the chihuahua. All he wanted to do was dress her in a unicorn onesie, pinch her cheek and say, 'You're my ickle cutie pop!'

'I've made my decision,' said the king aloud, patting her on the head. 'But you can always stay here with all the other trivial Wobbly Rock characters that don't have a starring role in this book, like Lady Mayfly, Henry the paper clip and Margaret Fluff the blacksmith.'

'How rude!' said Lady Mayfly, Henry the paper clip and Margaret Fluff the blacksmith.

Elle Emen-O'Pea put her arm around Betty. 'You've got to come,' she whispered. 'It wouldn't be the same without you.'

'Fine,' Betty grumbled, squashing her pride so far down it gave her a bellyache. 'I'll do it.'

'Now, say your catchphrase,' whispered the mouse.

Betty tried to pout but a little smile broke through.

'Say it . . .' the mouse repeated.

'All right, all right.' Betty let a big grin rise, and held her tweezers to the sky. **'LET'S GO LICK THE TOENAILS OF ADVENTURE!'**

SADDEST DAY OF MY LIFE

I came across a stunning fellow
A buzzing ball of black and yellow
But when I said, 'How do you do?'
He flew away and left me blue

by Clammy Pete

Not too sure about this one. I think Clammy Pete needs to get a life, if I'm perfectly honest. What do you think, reader? How many stars would you give it out of seventeen?

Chapter 3

 etty insisted on riding her handsome horse, Simon Anderson, all the way to Upper Crust, even though she looked like a plastic doll balanced on his massive noble saddle. Simon Anderson was admired far and wide for his glittering mane, tiger-print cycling shorts and the new cowboy boots Betty had given him for his birthday. **GOSH, HE WAS SO DISHY.**

The journey would last two days, taking them far

from the safety of Wobbly Rock. First, they would traverse the Forest of Dust, a dense woodland sparkling with pink pixie dust (not to be confused with the **TOXIC FOREST OF ETERNAL FIRE**, which is less *pixie vibes* and more **BLAZING INFERNO OF AGONY** *vibes*.) Next, they'd navigate the rocky paths that traced the Great Lakes of the Peckish Pilchards, before traversing the giant mushroom maze of the Fungal Jungle. Later, they would ride the Lonely Fields of Nothingness, stopping halfway for chicken nuggets at Tasty Joe's Cafe, before eventually crossing the Golden Gateway into the kingdom of Upper Crust.

'Make sure you stay at least five paces away from the water's edge,' said Figg, as the party made their way past the Great Lakes. 'Those pilchards would give their left earhole for a nibble on any one of us.'

Betty sighed. 'Yes, yes, we've all seen your **BUM.**'

Figg's BUM was his *Biweekly Unabridged Memo* – an informative document everyone had been instructed to read before leaving. Betty had actually taken a fair old glance at Figg's **BUM** the night before and felt pretty darn smug about it.

'And I think you'll find,' Betty continued, 'that the latest advice is to stay *six* paces from the Great Lakes. You might want to take a long, hard look at your own **BUM** once in a while.' She gave herself a high five for being such a **SMARTY FARTY EGGHEAD.**

Flying above Betty on the feathered back of Rupert Sometimes, Figg frowned and took a handful of notes from his bumbag to check if she was right.

Clinging on behind him, Elle Emen-O'Pea looked out at the landscape, holding her musical instrument tight. 'Never thought a simple mouse and her trumpet would see a sight like this,' she sighed happily.

As they reached the edge of the Fungal Jungle, Betty glanced back at the Great Lakes and took a big sniff of the pungent pilchard air. The afternoon

sun made the surface of the water glisten like a giant bowl of blueberry jam. Oh, it was a perfect peaceful moment. One of those moments that felt as though nothing scary or annoying could happen ever, ever again.

Just then, something scary and annoying happened. The peace was broken by a **CLONK**. Followed quickly by a **CLANG** and then a distinct **FLUMP**.

Betty scanned the Fungal Jungle for movement, poised to attack with her razor-sharp tweezers.

The royal carriage came to a halt. 'Boiled breadsticks!' said King Nutmeg, poking his head through the window. 'What's the hold-up?'

'Don't jolly worry, Your Majesty,' said Sir Loin of Beef, rubbing his lower back and thinking that he was getting too jolly old for this. 'We're just checking the area for critters.' Not only was his spine begging for a rest after so many years of gallant duty, but the massive wolf tattoo he'd secretly got when he was a young knight had never healed properly.

'Well, get a move on,' grumbled King Nutmeg. 'Pam and Pamm can't wait much longer for a bite of turnip, poor things.' Next to him, the twins held hands and whimpered bravely.

Betty narrowed her eyes and studied the enormous mushrooms. She knew there was something lurkin' in them. Then she glimpsed it.

Two strange, curved horns behind the head of a towering toadstool.

A thin white beard quivering in the shadows.

A high-pitched bleat soon echoed through the silence, followed quickly by an irritated, 'Shhh, Gilbert! We're supposed to be hiding.'

At once, Betty knew who they were dealing with. These fellas were the Gruff Goats. An infamous band of troublesome goats with sharp horns and stinky attitudes.

Betty summoned the strength of the trees, the power of the wind and the confidence of a really cool person in leather trousers. Then she flexed Linda and Gregg. 'Feeling strong, guys?' she asked.

Course they were! Linda and Gregg were at ninety-nine per cent power and eager to go. But Betty knew she needed one hundred per cent power if she was going to clobber this band of hairy bleaters. And that extra one per cent? Well, since becoming a mini version of herself, Betty had a new sure-fire way to boost her strength to the **MAX**. How, you ask? Two words . . .

Body spray.

Oh yes. Betty had started carrying a tiny can of the most potent underarm substance in the known universe. **BAD GAS.**

This famed scent was traditionally only reserved for the toughest of stag beetles and cockroaches, but Betty had chanced upon the rare toiletry on a recent revisit to the market of Brown Smudge. Sure, it had cost her a pretty penny, but – holy nostrils – it was worth it.

Betty took the can from her pouch and gave it a shake before spraying it under her pits. Oooooh-eeeee! It was spicy. It was musky. It was **BAD TO THE BONE.** At once, Betty knew she'd reached not merely one hundred per cent power, not even one hundred and one per cent, but a whopping **ONE HUNDRED AND FOUR PER CENT.** Golly gherkins, that's a lot!

The combination of Bad Gas and leather trousers was explosive. Betty sprang instantly into action. 'Watch out for the **GOATS!**' she cried.

'Oh, jolly crumbs!' shouted Sir Loin of Beef.

'I don't think I can do this,' stammered Johnny Logflume, fumbling with his custard-yellow flag.

'Where's your sword, boy?' snapped Sir Loin.

Johnny Logflume trembled and held the flag sideways like a giant, flappy weapon of destruction. 'I think I left it at home.'

Betty almost swooned at the sight of the masterful Johnny Logflume. But she knew she couldn't afford to get distracted. She had a job to do. Feeling fearsome, she yelled to the mushrooms:

'I KNOW YOU'RE IN THERE, YOU BEARDED BANDITS!'

'No, we're not!' came a high-pitched voice.

'Shhh, Gilbert!' whined another goat. 'Wait for the secret signal.'

'What's the secret signal again?' After a short pause, a loud sneeze emitted from the mushroomtops. 'Oh, was that it?'

'NO, GILBERT! FOR GOODNESS' SAKE. THAT WAS JUST SNEEZY STAN SNEEZING, AS USUAL. YOU KNOW HE'S ALLERGIC TO MUSHROOMS.'

Betty held up her trusty tweezers as she heard a long whistle.

'Now I remember!' came Gilbert's voice. 'The secret signal was a WHISTLE.'

What happened next was mega exciting.

Reader, just imagine your classic, run-of-the-mill goat ambush. Those baddies used all the usual tactics. I don't think I'll bother describing it to you, because I'm sure you know exactly what happened.

Anyway, the next morning, Betty made a cup of tea . . .

Hang on a minute, I've just had a letter.

Dear Salvador Catflap,

None of us here in the normal world have a bleedin' clue what a classic goat ambush is.

Yours impatiently,

Dave Schoolboy

Ah, I see. No problem. I'll describe it properly then.

STAGE ONE OF A CLASSIC GOAT AMBUSH:

 PROJECTILES

Perched on tall mushrooms, the ghastly goats threw down a load of potatoes. This sneaky trick is designed to disorientate the unsuspecting victims, so they go, 'Blimey, I wasn't expecting that!' But Betty Steady wasn't Betty Steady for nothing.

'Blimey,' she said proudly. 'I was **TOTALLY** expecting that!'

31

Our plucky gang dodged the raining debris with ease. Rupert Sometimes darted among the flying potatoes, while Sir Loin and Johnny Logflume used their exquisite swordsmanship and flagmanship to chop those spuds into French fries.

 STAGE TWO: BELLYFLOPPIN'

The goats leaped from the mushrooms and tried to inflict as much damage as possible with their furry little tummies. The Wobbly Rock crew did well to avoid the impact, although Elle Emen-O'Pea received a beard to the face and Pamm had to fend off a rogue horn through the carriage window.

TWACK!

As the rest of the gang began clonking the goats like nobody's business, Betty stayed perched on Simon Anderson and rummaged inside her satchel for a secret weapon. Just as a bewildered goat came charging towards her (this, incidentally, was Gilbert) she pulled out a large fishing net and made a plan. *Cartwheel. Forward roll. Lob the net over the grimy goats and tangle 'em up proper.* **DING DONG BELL!**

With one hand, Betty fended off the oncoming Gilbert with her tweezers. With the other, she swished the net high. With the other, she scratched her earlobe. Oh, wait, that doesn't add up. Forget the last bit.

Just as Betty was about to launch the net triumphantly over the grizzly goats, Sir Loin of Beef grabbed it from her.

'Look! A jolly net!' he announced.

Johnny Logflume took the other end. 'A net!' he repeated. 'Let's lob it over these grimy goats and tangle 'em up proper!'

'Jolly good idea!' said Sir Loin, hoping his back, with its sagging wolf tattoo, was up to the task.

Betty felt a pair of hands lift her from Simon Anderson's saddle and into the royal carriage.

'You'll be safe in here, little cupcake,' said King Nutmeg, setting her down next to Pam and Pamm and patting her on the head. 'Let the big boys sort out those nasties.'

Betty gritted her teeth.

'OH, HEAVENLY HANDS OF FATE!' she seethed, forced to watch Sir Loin and Johnny Logflume lob the net over the grimy goats and tangle 'em up proper. As the sound of defeated bleating echoed through her ears, she put her head in her hands and groaned. **IT'S NOT STINKING FAIR!'**

 hicken nugget?' asked Elle Emen-O'Pea, as the whole gang took a rest on the Lonely Fields of Nothingness with their takeaway boxes outside Tasty Joe's.

Betty shook her head, feeling angrier than a rhino in a traffic jam. She still couldn't believe Sir Loin and Johnny Logflume had taken **ALL** the credit for netting those ghastly goats. And worse, the king had completely dismissed her fighting

skills. And **WORSE** than worse, for some
unknown reason, the king had put her in a little
frilly hat.

Oblivious to her mood, King Nutmeg ate
his nuggets, immensely pleased with himself
for dressing sweet little Betty in Tiddles the
chihuahua's old bonnet. He couldn't believe his

luck when he found it down the side of the carriage door, along with a couple of twenty-carat diamond rings and half a packet of Hobnobs. He slapped Johnny Logflume and Sir Loin on the back. 'Great job back there, lads.'

'No jolly problem,' said Sir Loin, pretending his tattooed spine wasn't in agony.

'You should eat something, Betty,' said Elle. 'We'll be in Upper Crust soon, and you'll need all your strength to **PARTY YOUR FACE OFF!**'

Betty wasn't in the mood to party anything off. 'I'm always going to be a little cupcake to some people, aren't I?' she complained. 'However much Bad Gas I have, I'll always be tiny and pathetic.'

'Twaddle cakes,' said Elle Emen-O'Pea. 'You know, people used to tell me to give up the trumpet. They said I was just a **MEASLY MOUSE** with **LITTLE LUNGS**. But did I listen? Did I doughnuts!' She wiped her greasy paws and held up her instrument.

As Elle Emen-O'Pea began playing her award-winning masterpiece, *Fish Finger Boogie*, Betty could feel her shoulders relaxing. That mouse sure was talented. As the funky melody washed over the barren fields, Betty tried to pull herself together. She was here to enjoy herself, after all. And she was about to attend the coolest festival with the best band of buddies in the world.

Betty sniffed her armpits. Yep. She smelled like a winner, no matter what some people thought.

The remainder of the journey passed without incident – although Simon Anderson had to keep ducking behind the trees because, let's just say, the chicken nuggets didn't agree with him. But other than that, the royal party reached the Golden Gateway into Upper Crust on the second day as planned.

As Simon Anderson's noble cowboy boots took

their first steps under the glistening archway, he gave a dignified snort of excitement. (By the by, his cowboy boots really were somethin' special. Faux buffalo leather. Peacock feathers. Rhinestones aplenty. Betty had struggled to find him two matching pairs of such extravagant boots for his birthday, but she'd lucked out at a second-hand store called Hunky Stallions Boutique.) Betty's skin prickled too, her reddish-brown curls standing on end like excited caterpillars.

Compared to the boring grey kingdom of Wobbly Rock, Queen McNiff's realm was posher than a tiger in a top hat. The castle stood tall and proud, painted in the traditional purple spots you'd expect from such an important building. Rows of grand avenues guided them towards the palace, lined with rose bushes and trees trimmed into the shape of thumbs-up emojis.

Betty breathed in the clean air, which was set to a perfect twenty-one point six degrees. Above her, the birds tweeted in perfect harmony, performing a selection of well-known show tunes, while the butterflies whispered knock-knock jokes into the ears of passers-by.

Betty could feel herself drooling as she peered inside a swanky restaurant serving the finest cucumber sandwiches and cake pops known to humankind. All the Upper Crusters' drinks sported mini umbrellas or flags, which made Johnny Logflume hoot with joy.

This town had everything. Fashionable boutiques selling the most elegant silk gowns and hotpants. A twenty-four-hour emergency foot spa. A post office made of solid gold. And the public toilets? Well, let me assure you, they were FULLY stocked with loo roll.

These streets were so spotless that Rupert Sometimes was already looking forward to bin day. Naturally, Figg couldn't stop imagining the extensive town-planning paperwork. Simon

Anderson crossed his hunky legs, suddenly feeling the return of the nugget guts. Betty gave him a look which said, **NOT ON THESE SQUEAKY-CLEAN PAVEMENTS, YOU DON'T.**

Upper Crust was **PURE CLASS.** You might even say it was the bee's bottom. (Don't get too excited, Clammy Pete. That's just a phrase.)

When the travellers reached the castle, all they could say was, 'FNARPH!' No one knew what 'FNARPH' meant, but they soon forgot all about it when a team of frilly-shirted butlers greeted them. Much to Simon Anderson's dismay, he had to wait with the other horses in the stable (thankfully, his digestive issues seemed to have passed).

As the gang were shown around the castle, they all agreed that the artwork, tapestries and Magic Eye posters were the most elegant things they'd ever seen. That was until they got to the Great Hall and saw the turnips. **SUCH TURNIPS!** Turnips hanging from the ceiling. Turnips carved into

lanterns. Turnips arranged to spell 'TURNIPS ARE
PROPER TASTY' in big letters on the wall. There was
even a row of underpants above the fireplace, ready
for that evening, when the legendary Nanny Turnip
would climb up the toilet chute and leave festive
vegetable surprises for all the boys and girls.

At last, Queen McNiff strode into the hall,
followed by an imp with a clipboard. The graceful
queen wore a tall grey wig, embroidered robes
and a diamond crown. Although she had dainty
little features, her face was overpowered by her
eyebrows, which resembled big, hairy speech
marks.

'Your Majesty,' said King Nutmeg, with a bow.

Figg whispered, 'I told you, sire, that when two
monarchs meet, they're not supposed to bow. The
royal custom is to give the Special Gesture.'

'Yes, all right, Figg, all right.' King Nutmeg
grinned at Queen McNiff and, with utmost
elegance, pointed to his crown and said, **'SNAP!'**

43

Queen McNiff paused for a moment before cracking a gentle smile, pointing to her own crown and saying, **'SNAP!'**

'Such dignity,' sighed Figg, marvelling at the ceremonial tradition.

'I'm pleased you could make it, Nutters,' said the queen.

'Oh, it's a pleasure, Niffy,' said the king. 'A few days of vegetable shenanigans is just what I needed.'

'And, of course, some good-natured competition!' said the queen.

The king raised his eyebrows, which – although good – were nowhere near as handsome as Queen McNiff's. 'Competition?'

'You WILL be competing against me in the Royal Turnip Tournament?' said Queen McNiff, with a frown.

King Nutmeg didn't have the foggiest idea what she was going on about. 'Just remind me . . .'

'Three sporting battles,' said Queen McNiff. 'You versus me. Surely your advisor informed you of this noble and gruelling tradition?'

King Nutmeg scowled at Figg, who was deliberately looking down at his small green feet. Figg *had* read all about the tournament before they'd left, but after a night of one too many cherryades with Henry the paper clip, he'd **COMPLETELY FORGOTTEN** to tell the king. **HOW COULD HE EVER FORGIVE HIMSELF?**

'But never mind all that for now,' said the queen. 'You're just in time for my Turnip Eve speech.'

As the Wobbly Rock visitors took their seats by the throne, the queen nodded at two guards who opened the door. Hundreds of courtiers silently began filing in to the Great Hall and sat on the floor in rows facing the front. They crossed their legs, put their fingers on their lips and waited patiently. At the back of the hall, the eldest lords and ladies sat on special wooden PE benches because they were really grown-up and important.

'Good afternoon,' said the queen in a strict voice, her eyebrows drawn together for maximum impact.

Everyone stared at her hypnotic brows and replied, '**GOOD AFTERNOON, QUEEN MCNIFF. GOOD AFTERNOON, EVERYBODY.**'

The queen let her brows relax like two tired kittens. 'Now, I'm sure you're all looking forward to the Turnip Festival tomorrow.' A whisper of

46

excitement moved through the crowd. The queen sighed and said, 'Listening ears, please.'

The courtiers put their fingers back on their lips and sat up straight.

'But,' continued Queen McNiff, 'we must remember our **GOOD BEHAVIOUR.**' She picked up a pointing stick and held it up to a poster labelled **UPPER CRUST EXPECTATIONS.**

'Rule one: always say please and thank you.

'Rule two: no running around the castle.

'Rule three: no glittery nail varnish.'

'Superb regulations,' muttered Figg in a spiral of self doubt. Everything was so organised here. Compared to this, he was a Careless Colin. A Forgetful Freddy who hadn't told the king about the tournament. He didn't deserve to call himself an adviser.

Betty rolled her eyes. All these rules sounded like a bowl of twaddle cakes to her.

'And we must extend a warm welcome to our

47

esteemed guests from Wobbly Rock.' The queen gestured towards King Nutmeg. 'I know you will treat them with the kindness we expect here in Upper Crust.'

The queen cleared her magnificent throat.

'Turnip Eve is upon us,' she said. 'I hope you've all put your underpants out ready for Nanny Turnip. At this time of year, we must remember the true meaning of the Turnip Festival. Peace, Love and Carbohydrates. We all know the story of Nanny Turnip, the immortal being who grew underground in the dirt, brought alive by the magical power of Kindness. Every year, she blesses us by gathering vegetables and riding on her magical . . .'

'Impressive clipboard!' whispered Figg, as the queen's imp approached him. 'Standard A4. Retractable hook. Does it have a pen compartment?'

'Of course,' said the imp coolly. Her name was Plumm. 'And a stainless-steel clip.'

Queen McNiff held her hands high, as though Nanny Turnip was flying above her, and let her eyebrows go wild. **'HAPPY TURNIP EVE, ONE AND ALL!'**

The crowd applauded.

'Now, before we finish, I warn you that it's a little drizzly outside so it might be wet play.' The queen tapped her foot as everyone groaned. 'It's your time you're wasting . . .'

Finally dismissed, the court rushed home for their final Turnip Eve preparations. (Incidentally, Queen McNiff had given one of the butlers an Effie the Effort Elephant badge for improved candlestick polishing, which he couldn't wait to get home and show his mummy.)

'You'll be staying in the finest rooms in the palace,' Plumm told the Wobbly Rockers. 'Each suite has its own wash basin and chocolate fountain.'

'Fancy!' said Elle Emen-O'Pea, already excited to

hang up her underpants, ready for Nanny Turnip.

Plumm produced a set of shiny keys. 'King Nutmeg, you have been allocated Room One.'

'Splendid!' said the king, taking the first key and doing a happy little dance.

Plumm's green face showed zero appreciation of his funky moves. 'Princesses Pam and Pamm, you will take Room Two.'

Pam took the second key and tucked it safely in Pamm's armpit.

'And finally, Room Three,' said Plumm.

Betty shrugged. Room Three might not be the biggest, but it would surely do for a few nights of turnip fun. Plus, she couldn't wait to lay down on a

nice soft bed. But as she reached for the key, Plumm shook her tiny green head and pulled her hand away.

'*Room Three*,' said the Upper Crust imp, 'is reserved for the Royal Bodyguards, Sir Loin of Beef and Johnny Logflume.'

'WHAT IN THE NAME OF SHREDDED WHEAT?' Betty's voice echoed through the Great Hall.

Plumm checked her clipboard. 'You little ones are in the chicken coop.'

Betty's nostrils flared wider than a pair of doughnut holes. '*Little* ones?'

'Surely there's been a mistake?' said the king. He adjusted the bow under Betty's chin.

Betty sighed with relief. 'Thank you, Your Majesty –'

'This key says Yoga Studio,' said King Nutmeg.

'My sincerest apologies,' said Plumm, handing him the correct key.

Betty slapped her forehead. For one moment, she thought she was getting some stinking respect.

'Oh, and Betty?' said the king, holding up a pair of pink mittens. 'After you've settled into the chicken coop, you must try these on! They match your adorable hat!'

'Pink mittens?' cried Betty, throwing up her fists. **'THESE HANDS WERE MADE FOR BARE KNUCKLE FIGHTIN', NOT SISSY MITTENS!'**

'Steady on, Steady,' said the king, playfully shooing her away with his foot. He looked at Plumm. 'Sorry, she's a bit yappy today. Maybe she needs a treat.'

Betty snarled. 'Either I'm staying in a nice room or I'm unleashing Linda and Gregg.'

'Now, now,' said Plumm, with a hint of exasperation. 'We wouldn't want any trouble on Turnip Eve. I'm sure we can organise an upgrade.'

'There, little cupcake,' said King Nutmeg. 'No need to get your bonnet in a twist. You'll be sleeping soundly in a posh room before you know it.'

COMPLEX CREATURES

A colony of honey makers
Nectar drinkers, pollinators
Commanders of pernicious stings
A deadly swarm of stripes and wings
From raiding foe, the group survive
Emerging allied from the hive
Did you know that bees always go to the
supermarket on Wednesdays
So they can do the big shop while it's not too busy?

by Clammy Pete

OK. Weird. But you can't blame the bees, can
you? There's nothing worse than being stuck in a
long queue at the checkout.

 urnip Day! Turnip Day! **HOORAY, HOORAY FOR TURNIP DAY!** Golly gherkins, all the boys and girls were so excited to wake up at dawn to gorge themselves silly on vegetables. The Upper Crusters had three days of merry vegetable shenanigans to look forward to, culminating each evening in an exciting Royal Turnip Tournament event. **FNARPH!**

Much to her dismay, Betty didn't get to sleep in

a posh room. In fact, she barely slept at all, because the Crossword Crew had been relocated to the fish pantry, where the barrels of pickled herring were stored. I'm sure you can imagine the pong.

Betty woke up on Turnip Day feeling crosser than a hot cross bun. 'No one looks up to me any more,' she moaned, tossing her bonnet and mittens into a herring barrel. 'Doesn't that po-faced Plumm realise I'm the one and only Guardian of Wobbly Rock?'

Elle Emen-O'Pea was rifling through the underpants she'd left out for Nanny Turnip. **'YES!'** she cried. 'Two parsnips and a sprout!'

Betty grumbled, 'I get no darn respect from no one.'

'*We* respect you,' said Elle Emen-O'Pea, taking a nibble of parsnip.

Betty put her head in her hands. 'I've had it with being a stupid little cupcake.'

'Why don't we have one of our epic sleepovers tonight?' suggested Elle Emen-O'Pea. 'Maybe that will cheer you up.'

Betty's little heart was deflating like an old balloon. 'I'm not in the **STINKING MOOD,**' she growled. 'I want to go home!'

'At least join us for the breakfast buffet,' said Rupert Sometimes.

Upper Crust was known for its breakfast delicacy, the Royal Chef's stodgy bran flakes (rumoured to keep you extremely regular). This five-star banquet of bran was tempting, but Betty just wanted to sulk. She blew an angry raspberry in protest. **'NOPE. I'M OUTTA HERE.'**

Elle told Betty not to be silly and gave her a big, fluffy hug before leaving with the rest of the Crossword Crew for breakfast. Feeling thoroughly cheesed off, Betty climbed on to the window ledge and gazed out at the pink sunrise, which looked like a strawberry milkshake splattered in the sky. This place was supposed to feel like paradise, but right now it felt more like double detention with diarrhoea.

It simply wasn't fair. Hadn't she proved, time and time again, that she was still a fighting champion, even though she was small? So why was she being treated like a nappy-bum baby?

'Hey, what's your deal?' came a sudden voice from above.

Betty looked up to see a small sprite hovering outside the window.

'Are you talking to **ME?**' asked Betty, as the sprite fluttered closer.

'I don't see anyone else.' The sprite's wings were like sycamore leaves, and her hair was pink like candyfloss. Her dress, made from rose petals, was tied at the waist with gold ribbon. 'Are you human?' she asked, looking Betty up and down. 'You look human. But you're, like, tiny. No offence.' And she flicked back her bright pink hair.

'I'm only small because a stupid Toad Witch put me under a spell and **RUINED MY LIFE.**' Betty tried to flick back her own hair but her fingers got stuck in a tangle of curls.

'No way,' said the sprite, joining Betty on the windowsill. 'That's crazy beans.'

'Yeah,' said Betty. 'Like . . . a **WHOLE TIN** of crazy beans.'

The sprite smirked. 'I'm Misty Jamjar.'

Betty was suddenly very aware of her dirty fingernails and mucky tunic. 'I'm Betty Steady,' she said. 'The all-powerful Guardian of Wobbly Rock.'

Misty's eyes widened in surprise. 'Wow. Well, it's nice to see some new faces round here.'

'Hey,' said Betty, pleased that someone was finally taking notice of her. 'My gang are having one of our legendary sleepovers tonight. You should come.'

Misty looked interested. 'Sleepover? What kind of vibe are we talking?'

'Oh, we'll probably start with a good crossword,' said Betty, scratching her chin smugly because she knew she sounded seriously cool. 'Then my little mouse friend might play some funky tunes on her trumpet while we eat custard creams. Of course, we'll be up at the crack of dawn to watch the bin collection. Bin day must be so great here.'

'Bin day?' Misty Jamjar let out a hard laugh. 'Good one. You had me there for a minute.'

Betty furrowed her brow.

'Wait, you're being serious?' said the sprite. 'You

59

actually like trumpets and crosswords and bin day?'

Betty's cheeks turned pinker than a flamingo's lip balm. 'Um . . . no,' she said, scrambling around her brain for an explanation. 'Obviously, I'm **JOKING.** Crosswords are corny. Trumpets are terrible. And bin day is **BORING.'** She leaned her arm on the wall, trying to look unruffled. 'That's just the kind of crazy beans sense of humour we have in Wobbly Rock.'

'Oh right.' The sprite yawned and checked her sparkly nail polish (which was totally against the rules). 'Anyway, a bunch of us are meeting at Marsh Mellow Creek later. You can come too if you like. That is, if you're not hanging out with your own gang.'

Betty looked back into the fish pantry, at the stack of crossword puzzles and custard creams. It wouldn't hurt to try something new for a change, would it? After all, she felt like a stinky old **HAS-BEEN**, and her friends didn't seem to understand one bit. Maybe some *different* company would cheer her up and make her feel like her old self again.

'I'd love to,' she said, smiling at Misty Jamjar.

'LET'S GO LICK THE TOENAILS OF ADVENTURE!'

'Eww!' The sprite wrinkled her nose. 'Lick toenails?'

'JOKE!' said Betty. 'I meant, let's go . . . paint our toenails.'

'Ooh, yay!' said Misty. 'I've got the *best* sparkly polish.'

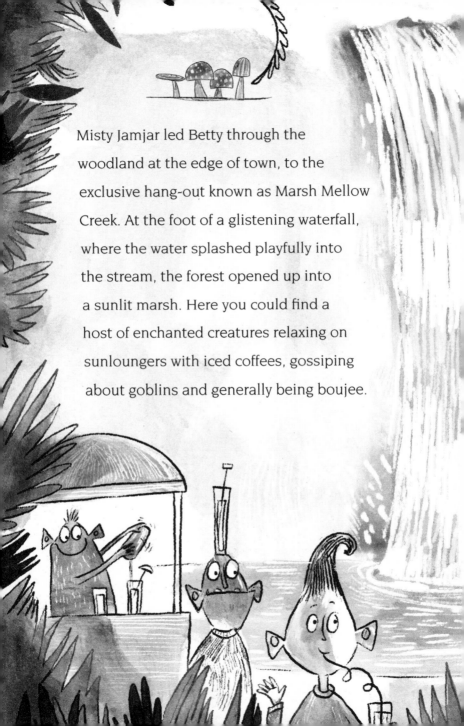

Misty Jamjar led Betty through the woodland at the edge of town, to the exclusive hang-out known as Marsh Mellow Creek. At the foot of a glistening waterfall, where the water splashed playfully into the stream, the forest opened up into a sunlit marsh. Here you could find a host of enchanted creatures relaxing on sunloungers with iced coffees, gossiping about goblins and generally being boujee.

It was the **PLACE TO BE** for the young sprites and pixies of Upper Crust.

Fascinated by this tiny new human in town, the little creatures greeted Betty enthusiastically. Betty's brain fizzed like a bath bomb.

'Pretty neat, huh?' said Misty. 'You should feel special. We don't invite just *anyone* here, you know.'

Betty felt special all right. This was just what she needed. Some stinking respect, **AT LAST.**

Everyone wanted to know what life as a prizefighter was like. And golly gherkins, Betty was more than happy to show off Linda and Gregg and give them all a sniff of her Bad Gas. After regaling the forest folk with tales of her heroic deeds, Betty felt like a **BIG CHEESE** again.

The afternoon sun beat down. Betty and Misty grabbed an iced coffee and took a seat on the riverbank.

'What was it like, being big?' asked Misty, coating Betty's pinkie toe with sparkly nail polish. 'I've always wondered.'

Betty closed her eyes and remembered the feeling of walking tall. 'People looked up to me,' she said. 'They respected me. And I could always reach the king's secret chocolate biscuit stash.'

'Unreal!' said Misty Jamjar. 'So would you change back? If you could?'

Betty thought about it. She *had* got used to being as tiny as a toilet roll. Enjoyed it, even. But over the last few days, things had changed. People were beginning to underestimate her incredible talents.

'You know what?' she said. 'Maybe I would.'

The sprite lowered her voice to a whisper. 'Then there *might* be a way I can help you,' she said.

Chapter
6

s Betty headed back to the castle, her head was spinning like a hamster wheel. Was there **REALLY** a way to reverse the grotty Toad Witch's spell and become tall and mighty again?

All around her, the festivities were in full swing as the spectacular Turnip Parade made its way through town. Vegetable-laden floats trundled over the cobbled streets. Giant Nanny Turnip puppets and tap-dancing onions wowed the crowds.

After dodging the large feet of a particularly enthusiastic onion dancer, Betty decided to hitch a ride on the back of a beetroot cart to save getting trampled. The bumpy journey scrambled her brain even further. Misty Jamjar had promised to explain the plan at the opening of the Royal Turnip Tournament that night, but Betty could hardly wait. **SHE WAS GOING TO BE A BIG, BEEFY BRUTE ONCE MORE!**

'There you are!' said Elle Emen-O'Pea, as Betty stumbled through the pantry door.

Rupert Sometimes glanced up from his newspaper. 'We were worried you'd gone home.'

'Change of plan,' said Betty, retching at the smell of herring.

The mouse clapped her paws. 'Oh, Betty. I'm pleased as pink pyjamas! I knew the promise of a sleepover would make you feel better!'

'I don't have time for a sleepover tonight.' Betty began rifling through her satchel for a comb and a tunic that didn't smell of fish.

'Of course you do!' said the mouse. 'After the Royal Turnip Tournament, we'll come back here for a **WILD** celebration.'

Rupert Sometimes put down his newspaper. 'I've found us a mind-boggling cryptic crossword to kick off the **PAR-TAY!**'

'Ugh, crosswords are corny,' Betty muttered under her breath.

'I beg your pardon?' said the owl.

Betty sighed. 'Nothing . . . Hey, we're going to be late for the tournament if we don't hurry.' She began changing into her cleanest tunic. 'Crazy beans late.'

'Crazy *what*?' said Elle Emen-O'Pea.

'You wouldn't understand,' said Betty. She took off her socks and checked her sparkly nails, which were still lookin' fabulous. 'Where's Figg?'

'Already at the arena,' said Rupert Sometimes. 'The king needed a little pep talk.'

68

Everything was set for the first round of the Royal Turnip Tournament, where the king and queen would battle it out in a game of Veg-e-table Tennis. This much-anticipated match would be played using the standard rules we all learned at school. Of course, reader, you love playing this classic sport in the normal world. So I'm certain you know exactly what I mean. In fact, I'm as sure as Nanny Turnip rides her magical –

Hang on. I've just got another letter.

Dear Salvador Catflap,

This is getting silly. WE OBVIOUSLY DON'T KNOW THE RULES OF VEG-E-TABLE TENNIS, YOU ABSOLUTE MUPPET.

Yours pulling-his-hair-outly,

Dave Schoolboy

Gosh. What **DO** you lot learn in school over there? Fine. I'll explain how to play Veg-e-table Tennis.

Players stand on opposite sides of a table, each wielding a metal sieve.

Opponents take it in turns to serve their vegetable, which must travel over the net and bounce in the other player's half.

Using the sieve, players lob the vegetable back and forth like a couple of happy hedgehogs, scoring points as they go.

After each point is scored, the vegetable is replaced by a larger variety, working up to the titans of the vegetable world – cabbages, cauliflowers and, in some particularly thrilling matches, pumpkins. (Warning: these heavy-duty vegetables are for professionals only.) First to score nine points wins. Simple really.

When Betty, Elle and Rupert Sometimes finally arrived at Upper Crust's world-renowned Green

Arena, the match was about to begin. The circular, open-air stadium, painted with green spots, seated hundreds of noisy Upper Crust spectators. At its centre, the Veg-e-table Tennis court was on full display to the hyped-up crowd. Pam and Pamm were sharing a shoe full of popcorn in the front row.

'Ooh, let's sit with the princesses,' said Elle Emen-O'Pea.

But Betty had spied Misty Jamjar on the other side of the arena, chatting with a stylish group of sprites. 'I'll join you in a minute,' she fibbed, slipping away from her friends.

At the centre of the arena, Figg was massaging King Nutmeg's shoulders. 'Remember to use a backhand volley on leafy greens,' he was saying.

'And put some spin on the root veggies.'

The king was sweating. 'My sieve looks wonky. **IS IT WONKY?!**'

'Deep breaths, Your Majesty. You can do this.' Figg was **DETERMINED** to make it up to the king for failing to inform him about the tournament. He'd been feeling terrible. What kind of an adviser forgets something so important? **HOW COULD HE LOOK HIS LAMINATOR IN THE FACE?**

As Queen McNiff entered the arena, the crowd roared. King Nutmeg's knees began to tremble. 'Quivering quail's eggs, Figg. I *can't* do this!'

Plumm approached Figg and the king. She narrowed her eyes. 'May the best monarch win,' she said.

Figg gulped.

Plumm pulled out her clipboard and positioned herself between the opponents. She coughed before raising her voice so that the entire arena could hear. **'QUEEN MCNIFF WILL SERVE FIRST.'**

King Nutmeg whispered to Figg, 'Great. Niffy's imp is the blimmin' umpire!'

'Don't worry, Your Majesty. I'll make sure she

adheres to the official regulations.' Figg pulled out his **BOOGER** (B*ook of Official Gala Event Rules*). 'Nothing gets past me.' The imp held it to his chest. By broccoli, he was going to make sure the king won this tournament. Then he'd be a worthy adviser once more. This **BOOGER** was the key to his **REDEMPTION.**

Meanwhile, Betty had found a seat next to Misty. 'Who do you think will win?' she said, slapping her thigh and letting out a howl of excitement. 'I love a **BRUTAL** tournament.'

Misty groaned. 'Ugh, I *despise* sport. I'm just here for the gossip.'

'Oh . . . yeah, me too.' Betty faked a yawn. 'Quite frankly, I'd rather watch spit dry.'

One of Misty's sprite friends leaned towards Betty. 'Do you know that imp down there? The king's dogsbody? He looks like **SUCH** a bore.'

'You mean Figg?' Betty felt an awkward prickle in her tummy, as though she'd eaten a cactus for lunch. 'He's . . . well, he *can* be dreary sometimes, I suppose.' The sprites all chuckled, and Betty's ego felt a little boost. 'Well, actually, he's duller than a filing cabinet!' she added. 'And he likes to hang out with a paper clip called Henry!'

Misty roared with laughter. 'Betty, you're *too* funny.'

As the tournament began, Betty tried to ignore the uneasy feeling that she was being a bad friend.

The crowd went silent as Plumm produced the first vegetable: a humble sprout. Handing it to the queen, the imp blew her whistle. **THE GAME WAS A KNEE.**

Wait. That's not right.

THE GAME WAS AN ELBOW.

No, that's not right either. What's the phrase again? Oh yes . . .

THE GAME WAS AFOOT!

The queen took a confident stance and launched the sprout into the air. Coming down hard with the sieve, she whacked the vegetable with force, sending it blasting over the net like a bolt of green lightning. Before King Nutmeg had a chance to react, the vegetable bounced off the other end of the table, landing with a plop in Pam and Pamm's popcorn shoe.

'ONE POINT TO QUEEN MCNIFF!'

cried Plumm.

The crowd went **BANANAS.** All except the Wobbly Rock gang, who went **PINEAPPLES** (which if you didn't know, is clapping politely

but not enthusiastically). And, of course,
the disinterested sprites around Betty went
LEMONS (which is no reaction whatsoever).

'Don't worry, Your Majesty,' Figg reassured the
king. 'You'll get the next point, I'm sure of it.'

King Nutmeg wiped a bead of sweat from his
forehead. 'She's got a killer swing, that Niffy.'

Plumm fetched the next vegetable. **'LADIES
AND GENTLEMEN,'** she shouted. **'THE
NAMESAKE OF THE FESTIVAL . . . THE**

**ICON OF THE VEGETABLE PATCH ...
THE ONE AND ONLY TURNIP!'** Handling
the purply-white vegetable with the respect it
deserved, Plumm passed it to King Nutmeg.

The audience started chanting, **'TURNIP,
TURNIP, TURNIP, TURNIP.'**

As King Nutmeg made his serve, Misty Jamjar
turned towards Betty and said, 'So . . . you want to
be tall again, huh?'

Betty felt a shiver down her little toe. 'Is there
really a way to change me back?'

Misty nodded. 'It won't be easy, but together
I think we can break into the queen's vault.'

'The queen's vault?!' Betty looked around to
make sure no one could overhear. 'Why would we
do that?'

Misty whispered, 'To borrow the Orb of Ogg.'

'The Orb of **WHAT?'**

Misty's eyes brightened. 'The Orb of Ogg is a ball
of light. Hidden in the dark depths of the vault, it

floats like a tiny, slumbering moon. Some call it the Sphere of Dreams. Others call it the Bubble of Weird Magic Stuff. All I know is that it has powers beyond compare. If you're looking for something to undo your shrinking spell, this is it, my friend.'

On the court below, the queen scored another point. And then another. But Betty was oblivious to it all. Lost in her imagination, she grasped the mystical Orb of Ogg, and returned to the fine specimen of high stature she used to be. No longer a little cupcake. No longer living in Pity City. Yes, siree, she had a one-way ticket to Beefcake Bay.

'So you're up for it?' asked Misty, as the queen aced another vegetable.

'Oh, I'm up for it,' said Betty. 'And I'm down for it. In fact, I'm turn-around-touch-your-toes-and-wiggle for it.'

'We'll need to get the master key from Plumm,' said the sprite.

'No problem,' said Betty.

79

'And the vault is Beverly guarded.'

'Don't you mean heavily guarded?' said Betty.

'Nope,' said Misty. 'It's protected by Beverly, the queen's most trusted Guard of the Vault.'

Queen McNiff took a honking great swing at a cabbage, winning the match in an impressive clean sweep. King Nutmeg threw his sieve on the floor. The game was well and truly over.

Betty's game, however, had only just begun.

'Well,' she said, with a broad smile. 'It seems this Beverly's got herself a date with Linda and Gregg.'

THIS POEM IS NOT ABOUT BEES

This poem is not about bees
There's nothing about bees at all
Instead it's about things like earmuffs and milk
And pelicans throwing a ball

And conkers and leopards and torn-up receipts
And pens, and the concept of bread
It's not about bees, not even one bit
So get those bees out of your head

This poem is all about twigs
And bus drivers smothered in jam
It's not about bees. It's NOT about bees
IT'S NOT ABOUT BEES, OK?

WILL YOU STOP THINKING ABOUT BEES,
FOR GOODNESS' SAKE?

by Clammy Pete

Gosh. I don't know what to say, really. Maybe the less said about this one, the better.

Chapter 7

he following day, the children of Upper Crust sang a lovely rhyme as they danced around the Turnip Tower (constructed every year from the town's sturdiest turnips). **'TURNIPS PLUMP AND TURNIPS ROUND, TURNIPS GROWING IN THE GROUND.'** Dressed in their frilly white gowns and vegetable bonnets, they whirled and twirled in the afternoon sun. **'TURNIP PIE AND TURNIP STEW,**

TURNIP CAKE FOR ME AND YOU. OBEY THE TURNIP OVERLORDS, DEFY THEM AT YOUR PERIL.'

Everybody clapped along to the jolly tune. It really was very sweet.

The traditional queen's picnic, which always took place on the second day of the festival, was well under way in the palace garden. In the lush royal grounds, beside the immaculate lawns, rose bushes and teetering Turnip Tower, a great feast was laid out. The fizzy pop flowed, the jellies wobbled and the sandwiches went a bit soggy in the heat.

Late to the celebrations, because she'd been up partying with Misty, Betty stopped off at the stables to fetch Simon Anderson. She'd barely seen her stunning stallion since she'd arrived, and she figured his gorgeous mane needed a good brush and blow-dry.

As she led him out of the smelly shed, she patted his soft coat. 'You don't belong in a stink pit,

you absolute dazzler.'

Simon Anderson took the chance to go for
a number two on the grass, because obviously
he wasn't going to do it in that manky stable.
Thankfully, the chicken nugget issues had passed,
so it was a very normal procedure. I assume you
all know how a horse goes for a number two, so
I won't bother explaining – actually, wait. I keep
getting those letters from Dave Schoolboy, don't I?
Well, I'm not making that mistake again. I suppose
you normal-world lot don't even know how a
horse goes to the toilet. Fine. I'll describe it in

meticulous, painstaking detail.

First the horse lifts its tail and holds its breath.

Then it squeezes – **OH, BOTHER, I'VE JUST GOT ANOTHER LETTER.**

Dear Salvador Catflap,

Of course we know how a horse goes to the toilet. And, quite frankly, it's not a very pleasant thing to think about.

You're really getting on my nerves now,

Dave Schoolboy

Fair enough. I'll leave it there.

So, after Simon Anderson had relieved himself, Betty led him to the picnic. 'Do you want to know a secret?' she whispered into his majestic ear. 'I'm going to be big again, my trusty steed. Just you wait and see.'

The horse gave an overjoyed neigh, before spotting a table of Scotch eggs and immediately tucking in. Trust me when I say he looked **STUNNING** with eggy crumbs tumbling through his bridle.

Elle Emen-O'Pea scurried towards Betty. 'Where in the name of fudge did *you* get to last night?'

Rupert Sometimes shook his head. 'You completely missed the bins this morning. It was exquisite.' He wiped a tear from his eye at the memory.

(A NOTE ON BIN DAY. Let me assure you, bin day in Upper Crust isn't just your standard smelly rubbish-truck situation. Picture the scene.

Bin butlers collect the refuse in golden carriages. White doves flit about, tying up the bin bags. The Royal Perfumier sprays a puff of sweet scent to disguise any lingering odours. Refuse collection had never been finer.)

Betty lay down in the sunshine and took a bite out of a sausage roll. 'Chill your chestnuts, guys. I had a late one last night and was **WAY** too snoozy to get up early. No big deal.'

'But you've *never* missed bin day!' said Rupert Sometimes. 'Even Figg was awake in time, despite staying up half the night studying that blasted **BOOGER.**'

Figg glanced up from his **BOOGER.** 'I've **GOT** to prove myself after my big blunder. And I can't let that hoity-toity Plumm get the better of me. I know the Royal Turnip Tournament rules inside out now. The king *will* win the gymnastics event tonight, let me assure you.'

'Betty!' came the sugary-sweet voice of Misty

Jamjar, as she fluttered towards the Crossword Crew.

'**MISTY!**' Betty gave the sprite a series of air kisses. 'Mwah, mwah, mwah!'

Figg, Rupert Sometimes and Elle Emen-O'Pea wrinkled their noses at each other, as if to say **THAT AIN'T OUR BETTY. NO, SIREE**.

'This is Misty Jamjar,' Betty told her pals. 'She's been showing me the sights of Upper Crust.'

Before they could continue the conversation, Queen McNiff clapped her hands in a fun little rhythm. Clap, clap, *clap-clap-clap*. The guests at the picnic knew to copy the beat. Clap, clap, *clap-clap-clap*. Immediately there was quiet and everyone looked up at the queen like good little children.

'Well done,' said the queen. 'You can all have a sticker.'

There followed a series of silent fist pumps.

'The Turnip Festival has been a scrumptious success so far,' Queen McNiff said. 'I do hope we're all looking forward to the second match of the Royal Turnip Tournament this evening. Nutters, I expect you've dusted off your leotard and pumped up your muscles. Swinging from the infamous Onion Rings isn't for the faint of heart!'

King Nutmeg, who had been enjoying a few pints of cherryade with Sir Loin of Beef and Johnny Logflume, gave a strained smile.

'Ugh, *boring*,' said Misty, rolling her eyes. 'Come

on, Betty, we've got to make a *plan*.'

'Woo-hoo!' Betty put down her sausage roll and jumped for joy. **'PAT-A-CAKE, PAT-A-CAKE, BAKER'S MAN!'** Even though breaking into the queen's vault was going to be a bit naughty, it was going to be **TOTALLY WORTH IT.**

'You're leaving again?' asked Elle Emen-O'Pea. 'But the Turnip Tombola's about to start!'

'Yuck!' muttered Misty.

'Yeah, gotta dash,' said Betty, trying to resist the temptation of an edge-of-your-seat tombola. 'But I'll catch you later. And let me just say, you might be in for a BIG surprise!'

'Fine. Be a Secretive Susan then.' Elle Emen-O'Pea fiddled with the bobble on her green hat. 'Just . . . look after yourself, OK?'

'What do you mean, *look after myself?*' snapped Betty. 'Oh, so now *you* think I'm a helpless little cupcake as well do you, *Tootsie Trumpet?*'

Elle's bobble hat went limp with sadness. 'No,

Betty, you absolute jam sandwich. That's not what I meant at all.'

Betty folded her arms. 'Things are gonna change round here, let me tell you. And maybe, just maybe, I won't have time for crosswords any more. How about *that*?'

Rupert Sometimes gasped. 'Take that back!'

Betty shrugged and clambered up Simon Anderson's tiger-print cycling shorts. **HOP ON, MISTY!'** she said, patting the saddle and brushing away a few stray eggy crumbs.

Misty flew up to join her new pal. 'It was nice to meet you,' she said, looking down at the Crossword Crew and sweeping back her flawless pink hair.

The Crossword Crew looked at each other and shook their heads, as if to say, **BETTY'S DUMPED US LIKE A BUNCH OF MOULDY FISHSTICKS.**

 t the Green Arena, in front of an eager crowd, Queen McNiff dangled from the Onion Rings. Suspended from two ropes, these famed vegetable hoops were made from the strongest onions (found only on the faraway shores of Shallot). Queen McNiff was no stranger to this spectacular gymnastic tradition, having trained since she was three days old. Consequently, she was confident as a candlestick.

For her first manoeuvre, she lifted her body effortlessly, sticking out her legs at a right angle. (A classic move.) Then she performed an aerial handstand, before bringing her legs down into an upside-down froggy pose. (Another classic move.) Finally, she attempted a Turnip Turnover, which is basically three and a half backflips performed in mid-air.

93

As she let herself glide to the floor, Queen McNiff was convinced she'd scored herself a perfect ten. But coming in to land, she *wobbled* a bit too much left, and *wibbled* a bit too much right. In her green leotard, she landed like a lime jelly, bobbing all over the place.

Plumm reluctantly held up a score of nine.

'Drat!' said the queen, her eyebrows bristling with frustration.

Next up was King Nutmeg. 'Be positive,' Figg advised, thumbing through his **BOOGER**. 'You can win if you perform the infamous Swede Somersault.'

The king tugged at his tight yellow leotard. 'Tumbling tangerines! I've never landed one of those!'

Figg looked him square in the eyes, determined to make amends for his forgetfulness. 'Your Majesty, it's the only way you can score enough points to beat the queen.'

94

Meanwhile, Betty and Misty were hiding behind a bin at the edge of the Green Arena. Carrying mops and dressed in overalls, they were about to undertake the first stage of their clever plan.

'Remember,' said Misty. 'If anyone asks, you're Tina.'

'Got it.' Betty tucked her curls inside a hairnet. 'Tina the Green Arena cleaner.'

'And I'm Gina. Gina the Green Arena cleaner.' Misty smoothed her pink hair into a bun. 'Are you ready, Steady?'

'I'm always ready, Jamjar. **LET'S GO LICK –**' Betty stopped herself. **'LET'S JUST GO.'**

Keeping their heads down, Tina and Gina the Green Arena cleaners made their way towards the judge's table just as King Nutmeg was beginning his routine on the Onion Rings.

As the nervous royal hung motionlessly from the ropes with arms like breadsticks, he looked down at Figg. 'I can't lift myself up.'

'Yes, you can,' said the imp. 'Think strong thoughts.'

King Nutmeg wrinkled his brow. 'Hmmm . . . What's strong? A hippo with a six-pack, that's pretty strong. Or maybe a bag of extra strong mints? No, that's stupid. Strong. Strong. Strong. Who's the strongest person I've ever met? Oh . . . I know! **BETTY STEADY!'**

As the king pictured Betty's powerful fists, he felt suddenly inspired. Although his biceps didn't have names, they managed to find just enough strength to lift him high. It was strange that the strongest person he could think of was a bonnet-wearing

little cupcake,
but he swept the
thought aside.

Now that he'd
finally managed
to heave himself
up, the king
had enough
momentum to
complete his first
move. As he turned
upside down and
did the splits, the
crowd *oohe*d and
*ahhe*d. Then he
brought his knees
up and did bicycle
legs while the
crowd *wowe*d and
*blimey*ed.

At the judge's table, Plumm was looking on with a face like a wet welly. She didn't notice the two fake cleaners mopping the floor behind her. Tina and Gina the Green Arena cleaners inched closer, ready to strike.

King Nutmeg psyched himself up for the Swede Somersault. Taking a deep breath and making a plea to the **HEAVENLY HANDS OF FATE,** he launched into the move. To the amazement of the audience, he spun in the air like a graceful gibbon. Twist. Turn. Star jump. Robot arms. A textbook Swede Somersault.

Just as he was about to land, Plumm let out a deliberate sneeze. Startled by the noise, the king lost his balance and landed on his rear end with a bump.

Plumm swiftly held up a score of eight.

'Not so fast,' said Figg, smooth as a currant bun. 'I think you'll find that rule seventy-two in the official regulations states that any sudden expulsion of air or gas from a spectator voids the move.' He slammed his **BOOGER** on the table. 'The contestant is permitted a second attempt.'

'I believe you're mistaken,' said Plumm, her green cheeks turning to red like a traffic light.

Figg tapped the book. 'Read it and weep, sneezer.'

'Fine,' Plumm said through gritted teeth. 'The king may reattempt the move.'

Figg felt a glimmer of joy in his little green heart. Perhaps he *could* be a worthy adviser again.

The king rubbed chalk on his hands. **'BE. LIKE. BETTY,'** he told himself.

As he got into position, his chest rattled like a stoat trapped in a lunchbox, but he took a deep breath and channelled Betty's strength. Soon he was whirling and whizzing through the air like nobody's business. A nimble noble of the sky. A limber leader of the air.

The crowd held their breath. Figg held his **BOOGER.** Simon Anderson held in a trump.

99

(Although he was outside the arena so nobody would have noticed.)

Under immense pressure, King Nutmeg somehow landed the Swede Somersault perfectly.

Everyone went loopy. Pam jumped on Pamm's back and started a chant of **'BOOGLE-OOGLE-BLIM-BLAM!'**

In all the commotion, Tina and Gina the Green Arena cleaners crept up behind Plumm. While Gina diverted her with some vigorous mopping action and a comment about a sticky patch, Tina bent down and swiped the master key from the imp's keychain.

'LITTLE MISS MUFFET!' said a triumphant Betty. I mean, Tina.

As Plumm comforted a disappointed Queen McNiff, Gina and Tina took their chance to scurry away into the crowd. Loud cries of **'BOOGLE-OOGLE-BLIM-BLAM!'** carried across the arena. The citizens of Upper Crust were well and truly won over by King Nutmeg's spindly-legged splendour. Even when Queen McNiff did her clap, clap, *clap-clap-clap*, everyone carried on celebrating as the king postured and posed for the admiring mob.

'**THAT'S ENOUGH!**' shouted the queen, her eyebrows shooting a metre into the air.

Now they knew she meant business.

Quiet filled the arena and everyone looked rather sheepish. But little did the queen know that Betty and Misty were already on their way to the palace, to face the Beverly guarded vault – and steal the Orb of Ogg.

BUZZ (Original Bee Version)

Buzz, buzz, buzz.
Buzz* buzz?
Buzz! (Buzz buzz).
"Buzz," buzz Buzz.
Buzz@buzz.buzz
*Buzz

by Clammy Pete

Unfortunately, I don't speak bee, so I haven't the foggiest idea what this poem is about. We were taught dragonfly at school, which I'm pleased to say I am fluent in. However, if there are any budding buzzers out there, please feel free to translate!

imon Anderson's cowboy boots clip-clopped over the cobbles towards the castle. Tugging on his reins, Betty prayed that Beverly, the queen's most trusted Guard of the Vault, couldn't hear them approaching.

As luck would have it, Beverly couldn't hear much at all because she was humming a little tune to herself. I bet you think that makes her sound wimpy, but the song was called **'I LIKE BIFFIN'**

THIEVES IN THE NOGGIN'.

Let me tell you a bit about Beverly.

She was five foot one of pure muscle. Arms like fire extinguishers, thighs like cement mixers, abs like speed bumps . . . and a load of other brilliant similes I don't have time to write because my mum said I have to do the washing-up.

Oh, Beverly.

She wore a black catsuit studded with spikes. She carried an axe called Choppy Bob. (Coincidentally, her hair was styled in what's known in the hairdressing game as a 'choppy bob'.)

Whoa, Beverly.

She could bench-press twelve Shetland ponies. She could snap a radiator in half just by looking at it. Yep, this woman was tough with a capital B. And tough doesn't even have a B. That's just how tough she was.

Beverly had been guarding the queen's vault every night for seven years, except for one random Tuesday when she accidentally went to a roller disco. But otherwise, she was always there and always ready to fight off any wrong'uns who dared try to steal from the queen.

And a couple of wrong'uns were on their merry way.

Betty and Misty tied Simon Anderson outside the palace, ready for a speedy getaway.

'I hope you're feeling strong,' Betty told her stallion. 'Because next time you see me, I'll be **HULKY** and **BULKY.'**

Simon Anderson raised a gorgeous eyebrow, as if to say, **BETTY, MY SADDLE CAN TAKE THE WEIGHT OF A THOUSAND SHOPPING BAGS. AND NOT PATHETIC SHOPPING BAGS FILLED WITH THE EASY BITS, LIKE BREAD AND CRISPS. NO, THE PROPER WEIGHTY STUFF, LIKE MILK AND ORANGE SQUASH. THE TYPE OF BAGS THAT LEAVE PAINFUL LINES ON YOUR HANDS WHEN YOU CARRY THEM IN FROM THE CAR.**

Betty nodded knowingly.

'This way!' whispered Misty, flying up to a high window. 'Hurry.'

Betty climbed Simon Anderson's reins, scaled the wall and scrambled on to the window ledge. She found herself in a shadowy hallway lit by candlelight. Misty led the way through a series of dark passages, past the empty yoga studio and up a winding staircase. Finally, the pair came to a big steel door where **THE WOMAN HERSELF** was waiting.

'We're here to borrow the Orb of Ogg!' Betty declared. 'So get out of our way, if you know what's good for you!'

Beverly held Choppy Bob and sneered. She looked Betty up and down, which didn't take long because she was the height of a cheese toastie.

'You think you can get past me?' she said in a voice that sounded like she had dry Weetabix stuck in her throat. 'What a silly little goose!'

Betty laughed. 'This silly little goose is about to **ANNIHILATE YOU!'** Then she did her tried and tested battle ritual: leather trousers, Bad Gas, the lot. She was at **ONE HUNDRED AND FOUR PER CENT POWER** and raring to go.

As Misty Jamjar kept her distance, Beverly raised

Choppy Bob and brought him down with a **WHACK**.
Betty did a cartwheel and dodged the blade.

'Oh, you're a *sneaky* little goose!' Beverly raised
her axe for another **WHACKING!**

Betty ran towards the vault door and bounced off
the frame with a twist, landing on Beverly's burly leg.
Quicker than a chimp playing tag, she climbed up
the spikes on Beverly's catsuit, avoiding the guard's

swiping hands. Linda and Gregg were working overtime! When Betty reached her shoulders, she dodged Choppy Bob, grabbed a hairy clump of choppy bob and swung on to Beverly's nose. Then she yanked the guard's bushy nostril hairs with her tweezers.

'Yikes!' cried Beverly. 'You're a *nasty* goose!'

'Watch out!' cried Misty.

Betty looked around to see Beverly's fist coming straight for her. Like the absolute champion she was, she somersaulted to the floor. Beverly accidentally gave herself a clonk on the nose, but she rubbed it better and composed herself. **'COME ON THEN, GOOSEY!'** she yelled.

Betty glanced up at Misty Jamjar. 'Does she actually think I'm a goose or something?'

Misty shrugged.

'WHATCHA WAITIN' FOR?' asked Beverly, swishing her choppy bob hair about as though she'd just walked out of the salon. Betty had to admit, it was a striking hairdo. But she wouldn't let herself be dazzled by its defined layers.

She jumped to her feet and held up her fists. **'GOOSEY WANTS TO PLAY!'**

Beverly narrowed her eyes. **'GOBBLE, GOBBLE!'**

'No, that's a turkey,' said Misty.

'Oh.' Beverly put down her axe. 'What noise does a goose make?'

'Do they quack?' asked the sprite. 'Or maybe they hiss.'

'No, I think they honk,' said Betty.

'Fine.' Beverly got back into position. **'HONK, HONK!'**

'HONK, HONK!' said Betty, squaring up to the Guard of the Vault. 'Now, let's get down to business. My sprite friend and I are going to use that magic orb thing you've got hidden in there. We're not real baddies or anything, so we're going to put it right back. No one even needs to know we've been here.'

'You're not getting anywhere near the Orb,' said Beverly.

'We can do this the easy way or the hard way,' said Betty. 'Or the medium way.'

'Nope. We're doing it *my* way.'

Beverly lunged for Betty, but Betty rolled away like a cheeky tomato. The guard whirled Choppy Bob once. **THWACK!** Twice. **WALLOP!** Three times. **KACHONG!** Betty sidestepped 'em all, **EASY-PEASY.** She ran through Beverly's legs ready to bolt for the vault door – but just as she picked up speed, the Guard of the Vault grabbed her and lifted her with her meaty hands, licking her lips.

'MUMMY'S COOKED A GOOSE FOR SUPPER!'

Betty wriggled and squirmed. **'I'M NOT A GOOSE!'**

'That's just what a **LYING LITTLE GOOSE** would say!' Beverly brought Betty up in front of her big face. 'You're in a **LOT** of trouble, missy.'

'No, **YOU'RE** in a lot of trouble!'

Betty kicked off her boot and revealed her fabulous feet. Tilting her toenail so it reflected the candlelight, Betty made her sparkly nail polish twinkle like crazy. Beverly was blinded by the overpowering glittery splendour. She winced and loosened her grip, giving Betty enough room to reach into her bag and pull out a rope.

'GRAB THIS, MISTY!' Betty cried, throwing one end of the rope to the sprite.

But the sprite fumbled the catch. 'Whoops.'

'No problem,' said Betty. **'I GOT THIS.'** She looped the rope round the guard's wrists, then bungee-jumped to the ground. Channelling her inner maypole dancer, she began swirling around Beverly, wrapping the guard in rope so she couldn't move.

'Oi!' cried Beverly, as Betty shimmied up the door frame and tied the rope to the handle.

'That should hold her,' said Betty, dropping to the ground and kicking the axe out of Beverly's reach. Then she took out the key she'd stolen from Plumm. 'Orb of Ogg, here we come.'

Beverly sighed, flicked her choppy bob out of her eyes and peered over to her axe. 'Beaten by a silly little goose! Oh, Choppy Bob, we'll never live this down!'

ow!' said Betty. 'It's magnificent!'

'It's so cool!' said Misty.

'Anyway,' said Betty, 'we should probably stop looking at Beverly's hairdo and go find the Orb of Ogg.'

'Good idea,' said Misty.

The pair made their way into the vault, leaving Beverly tied to the door. There in the darkness were the queen's most valuable possessions – jewels, gems, diamond-encrusted jogging bottoms. The most precious object of all was kept far at the back, behind a velvet drape with a sign that read: **ATTENTION, ROBBERS! THERE'S NOTHING TO SEE BEHIND THIS CURTAIN SO DON'T EVEN BOTHER LOOKING.** But Misty was wise to this clever security system and pulled the curtain open anyway.

'Whoa!' said Betty, shielding her eyes from the light. 'You're well smart!'

There it was, floating like a spooky bowling ball. The Orb of Ogg.

Rumour had it, the Orb of Ogg had been created thousands of years ago in the distant Land of the Fidgety Wizards. Born of fire and gemstone when someone accidentally dropped their belly-button ring in a toaster, it had powers beyond understanding. Queen McNiff kept it locked away in case anyone used it to do something silly. Betty, of course, would never do *anything* silly.

'I want to lick it,' said Betty. 'It looks like a big blob of ice cream.'

Misty shook her head. 'Don't be daft. We need to carry it outside *really* carefully.'

'Outside?' said Betty. 'I thought we were going to keep it in here?'

'The magic works better by moonlight,' said the sprite. 'But don't worry, we can *totally* return it once we're done.'

Betty didn't like the thought of actually *taking* the Orb of Ogg. That felt quite a lot like stealing, not borrowing. She couldn't help picturing Figg's disappointed face. In fact, she could almost hear him whispering his favourite saying: **THE TWO MOST IMPORTANT THINGS IN LIFE ARE CLEAN PANTS AND NOT STEALING.**

'I'm not so sure,' said Betty, with a guilty gorilla rattling around her brain. 'Wouldn't this make me a baddie? I **HATE** baddies.'

Misty sighed. 'Don't be such a little cupcake, Betty.'

Betty clenched her fists. She'd had enough of people calling her that. This was **IT.** She wasn't staying a little cupcake **ONE SECOND LONGER.**

More determined than ever, she climbed up the curtain and grabbed the Orb of Ogg.

In a secluded spot outside the castle, Betty nervously held the Orb of Ogg above her head. Although it was enormous in her little hands, it was

as light as a helium balloon, and gave off a fizzy
kind of energy, like lemonade.

'**I'M FREAKING OUT,**' she said, at the
thought of what she was about to do. '**TEN
GREEN BOTTLES! LITTLE BO PEEP!
OLD MACDONALD HAD A FARM!**'

'Pull yourself together,' said Misty, sounding
bored. 'Before anyone sees us.'

Betty glanced up at Simon Anderson, who gave
her an encouraging and incredibly handsome nod.

'Orb of Ogg,' she whispered, imagining how
strapping she was about to become. 'Mystical ball
of . . . erm . . . magic goo. Grant my wish . . . Reverse
my curse . . . **JUST MAKE ME BIG AGAIN!**'
She closed her eyes, waiting for something to
happen. '**PLEASE?**'

Just as the Orb began to shake, she had the
sudden realisation that she'd no longer be able to
cuddle her little pals without squishing them. But it
was too late to worry about that.

110

The Orb blasted apart in an explosion of white. Betty felt lightning through her fingers and thunder through her toes. Her skin cracked like dry mud. Her arms and legs stretched like stringy cheese. Then everything went dark.

The next thing Betty was aware of was a wet sensation on her face. She groaned and opened her eyes. Simon Anderson was licking her cheek.

'Smokin' saddlebags!' she said, her body aching. 'That was really weird.'

She was still holding the Orb, which was whole again, but it felt different. Smaller in her hands.

No, wait. The *Orb* wasn't smaller.

Betty was bigger.

She leaped up. **IT WORKED! I'M ME AGAIN!'**

Simon Anderson did a little tap dance with his swish boots.

'Whoa, that's crazy beans!' Misty fluttered around, gazing in awe at Betty's full-size frame. 'How do you feel?'

'I FEEL GREAT!'

Betty admired her long legs and mighty fists. But before she had a chance to check if Linda and Gregg were pumped up to perfection, Misty snatched away the Orb of Ogg.

'My turn!' shouted the sprite.

Betty was baffled. 'Wait, you're going to make yourself bigger too?'

'Duh!' said the sprite. 'Why do you think I'm here?'

'I thought you just wanted to help me,' said Betty. She suddenly had a really stinky feeling about this.

'Well, actually, I needed *your* help to get past Beverly. I couldn't do any of that fighty stuff.' Sniggering, the sprite flew to a high tree branch and held up the Orb. 'But now that I've got this,' she said, 'I can do anything I want. **OMG,** Queen McNiff is going to be **SOOO** sorry!' She gave Betty a mysterious smirk, then held up the Orb.

'GREAT AND POWERFUL ORB OF OGG . . . MAKE ME MASSIVE!'

Betty gasped. How could she have trusted Misty? She'd been up to no good this whole time! Betty had to do something *crazy beans* fast.

As the Orb began to glow, Betty launched into

battle mode. First, she did a cartwheel (nearly hitting Simon Anderson in the face because she wasn't used to having such long legs). Then she swung from a low branch (snapping it in two because she was so hefty). Then she ate a packet of Hula Hoops, which were **WAY** smaller now she was so big – no, wait. It was Simon Anderson who ate them. Anyway, Betty had her hands on that Orb before you could say *salt and vinegar*.

'Get your dirty fingers off my Orb,' spat Misty.

'No **STINKING** way!' Betty cried, enjoying the incredible power of her human-sized limbs.

Misty was still the size of a tiddly teabag, so burly Betty was able to prise the Orb away from her, easy as scrambled eggs. But unfortunately, the spell had already been cast. As the Orb exploded with light all over again, the magic that was meant for Misty . . . hit *Betty*.

In a fog of wibbly-wobbly weirdness, sparks began to shoot through Betty's veins. Her cheeks inflated like balloons. Her stomach swelled like a souffle. Her limbs flung apart like a pop-up tent. Then, just as the ground beneath her seemed to be moving away, everything went dark again.

THE PARTY

I wore a fluffy yellow coat
Borrowed from my mum
Fastened on a pair of wings
And taught myself to hum

Then Friday evening, all prepared
A little after five
My mother told me I looked swell
And walked me to the hive

I was such a handsome bee
According to my mummy
I blended in quite perfectly
And tried a bit of honey

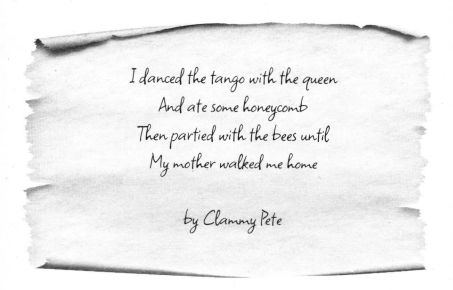

I danced the tango with the queen
And ate some honeycomb
Then partied with the bees until
My mother walked me home

by Clammy Pete

Well, it's got something, hasn't it? Not necessarily something good. But still. It's got something. What do you reckon?

Chapter 11

he scent of freshly-baked bran flakes wafted from the palace kitchens, stirring Betty awake. She groaned. What had *happened* last night?

Then the memory hit her like a soggy sardine.

'I've been an absolute jam sandwich,' she said to herself, sitting up and rubbing her eyes. She was still outside the castle, where Misty had attempted to use the Orb for some sort of shifty plan. But the sprite was nowhere to be seen. And neither was the Orb.

In a tired haze, Betty could swear there was a small animal tickling her foot. 'Get off,' she said, flicking it away with her pointy boot. Then she heard a familiar neigh.

'**SIMON ANDERSON?!**' she gasped. '**IS THAT YOU?!**'

Betty's eyes nearly popped out of her nostrils. Her stallion was **TINY.**

Simon Anderson gave her a serious stare. A stare that could only mean one thing. **IT WAS TIME TO BRAID EACH OTHER'S HAIR!** Oh no, wait. It probably meant something else, actually. Maybe something like, **NO, BETTY, YOU'VE GOT IT WRONG. I'M NOT TINY! YOU'RE BLOOMIN' MASSIVE!**

Betty looked down at her body. The horse was right. She was **ENORMOUS.** Woozy and confused, she stood up to find that the treetops only came to her shoulders. And if she stretched her arms, she could reach the top of the castle.

'I'M A GIANT!' she cried. 'WHY AM I A GIANT?!'

Betty bent down and picked up her loyal horse. He looked like a little kitten there in her palm, and she was suddenly overcome with the desire to dress him up in a fuzzy unicorn onesie. Wait. Was this how King Nutmeg had felt about *her*? But she shook the thought away and instead placed him on her shoulder like a cool pirate. Golly gherkins, he looked good up there.

'Misty's **MAKE ME MASSIVE** spell must have wormed its way into me when I took the Orb from her,' said Betty. 'Now I've had a double dose of magic and I'm taller than a giraffe in high heels.'

How had it all gone so wrong so quickly? Betty longed to see her beloved Crossword Crew and tell them everything. But how could she face them? How could she explain what she'd done? And most importantly, how could she fit through the fish

pantry door?

'Oh, I was a right Gullible Gladys,' Betty groaned.
'That sprite tricked me good and proper.' She
turned to Simon Anderson. 'I was a terrible friend
to the gang, wasn't I?'

The horse nodded.

'I don't know what I was thinking. **I LOVE
CROSSWORDS!** They're not corny at all.
They're the coolest thing since sliced cheese,' said
Betty glumly. 'I've got to make it up to them.'

Betty crouched outside the fish-pantry window,
pushing the twigs out of her eyes. She'd stuck a few
branches in her hair so she resembled a huge tree:
a surprisingly effective disguise.

'Betty didn't come back last night,' Rupert
Sometimes was saying, his spectacles fogged with
tears. Betty's heart felt as heavy as a washing machine.

Elle Emen-O'Pea gave a mousey sigh. 'We're *old*

130

news to her now. *Yesterday's loo roll.'*

Betty took an ashamed step back from the window but continued to listen in.

'Have I got *something* to tell you!' came Figg's voice, as he burst through the door and unzipped his bumbag.

'Figg?' said Rupert Sometimes. 'Where have you been? *You're* not doing a Betty on us now, are you?'

'Actually, I've been in the palace library, doing a little digging on Misty Jamjar.'

'Oh, spill the gravy!' said Elle Emen-O'Pea.

'According to the palace records,' said Figg, 'Misty used to work at the castle. She was the Royal Hair, Make-Up and Tax Specialist. The queen adored her! Treated her like the daughter she never had. Until Misty began pushing her luck.'

'I knew she was trouble,' said Rupert Sometimes.

'Apparently,' said Figg, 'she held a wild party for her sprite friends and trashed the Great Hall. Then, during one of the queen's speeches, she yawned and loudly announced that she'd had more fun changing a duvet cover. But the last straw came when the queen noticed some inconsistencies in the tax accounts. It turned out, Misty had been awarding herself a little pocket money.'

Elle Emen-O'Pea and Rupert Sometimes gasped like two old ladies watching a scary movie.

'You know how the queen expects the rules to be

obeyed,' Figg continued. 'She was furious and threw Misty out of the palace. Very publicly.'

Betty gulped. So that's why Misty had been all revengey. And she'd only gone and helped her steal the most powerful weapon in Upper Crust. Whoops times a million.

'Blimey, we need to tell Betty about this,' said Elle Emen-O'Pea.

Betty wanted to let them know she was listening. She wanted to hold them tight and say she was sorry for being the biggest jam sandwich in the sandwich shop. But the **ALL-POWERFUL SAUSAGE OF SHAME** was holding her back. She couldn't face the Crossword Crew until she'd put things right.

'Listen up, Sally Sunshine,' she said to Simon Anderson, perched on her shoulder. 'We're going to find that crafty sprite and return the Orb of Ogg!' Betty stood tall and put her hands on her hips. **'OPERATION PUT THINGS RIGHT IS GO!'**

Simon Anderson neighed in solidarity.

'Oh, and I just remembered that I need to turn myself back to my normal height before I return the Orb. Because, you know, I'm ridiculously humongous and won't be able to find any clean pants to fit.' Betty snapped her massive underwear. **'OPERATION PUT THINGS RIGHT IS GO!'**

Simon Anderson roared with loyalty.

'Oh, and one more thing. I should probably untie Beverly from the vault door. She'll need a wee by now.' Betty pulled an impressively courageous face. **'OPERATION PUT THINGS RIGHT IS –'**

Simon Anderson interrupted her with a very loud grunt which meant **JUST GET ON WITH IT.**

Chapter 12

nce Betty had freed Beverly (by sticking her long arm through the castle window, reaching down the hallway past the yoga studio and untying the rope), she knew the queen's guards would be after her soon enough. Not to mention Choppy Bob.

Time was of the essence. Betty had to find Misty Jamjar and the Orb of Ogg without delay! She did, however, decide to stop briefly for some bran flakes because you can't fight on an empty stomach. And she found she was a little hungrier than normal, being bigger than a house. So instead of her usual small bowl of cereal, she filled a rusty skip with milk and chowed down, using a stop sign as a spoon. A modest snack to see her through until lunchtime.

Yes, Betty had an enormous body. But she also had an enormous *brain*. And that brain knew just where to look for Misty Jamjar. The fishmonger's!

'TO THE FISHMONGER'S!' said Betty.

Then she remembered that Upper Crust didn't actually have a fishmonger's. So she double-checked with her enormous brain, which thought really hard and came up with another idea. Marsh Mellow Creek!

'TO MARSH MELLOW CREEK!' said Betty, making her way to Misty's favourite hang-out.

But she was in for a surprise. Chaos was waiting for her . . .

'Hi, I'm Chaos,' said a random pixie doing a spot

136

of knitting. 'I've been waiting for you.'

'Oh, right,' said Betty. 'Nice to meet you. So what's been going on?'

'Mayhem!' said the pixie. 'Mayhem, come over here!' Carrying a bundle of yarn, another pixie flew towards them. 'Mayhem, tell Betty what Misty Jamjar's been up to.'

Mayhem sat down and took out her knitting needles. 'It's been awful! We were having a lovely time, when Misty unexpectedly shows up and shouts, **MAKE ME MASSIVE!** Then she suddenly becomes all huge, like you, deary. And she's got this big, shiny ball thing.'

'Orb of Ogg,' said Betty.

'Cover your mouth when you cough, please,' said

Mayhem, looping the wool around her needle.

'No. The shiny ball thing is called the Orb of Ogg.'

'Oh. Well, she had this . . . Org of Obb . . . thingy and announced that she was going to *ruin the queen's stupid, boring Turnip Festival*. And whoever wanted to join her had to come to the Green Arena to *wipe the smile off Queen McNiff's stuck-up face*.' Mayhem tugged sharply on her yarn. 'Well, of course, all us sensible pixies said no. We like a peaceful life. But the sprites? Let me tell you, deary, they didn't take much persuading. And guess what? All of a sudden, she does another spell and makes the sprites massive too.'

Now, reader, I assume you know all about the mischievous behaviour of sprites. Or maybe you don't. I keep doubting myself because of Dave Schoolboy's blinking letters.

Oh, for goodness' sake. I've just received *another* envelope. How are these letters even getting here? Don't they have to travel through time and space?

Anyway. Let's see what know-all Dave has to say this time.

Dear Salvador Catflap,

Your order for five pairs of heart-print underpants has been received and will be delivered in five working days.

Thank you for being a loyal customer,

The Big Comfy Pants Company

Ahem. Moving on.

So the thing about sprites is that they *love* a bit of drama. Can't help themselves. And they're easily led, too. If someone like Misty shows up with a nasty plan, chances are they're going to jump at the chance to join in just for the thrill of it. Even if they don't have a clue why.

Betty had a duty to protect the queen. After all, it was her fault Misty was loose with an all-powerful orb. And if the sprite was going to cause trouble at the Royal Turnip Tournament, that meant Betty's buddies were in danger too.

There was no choice. The Guardian of Wobbly Rock had to become the Guardian of Upper Crust. (For a limited time only.)

Betty left Chaos and Mayhem at Marsh Mellow Creek and got ready to face chaos and mayhem at the Green Arena. 'Come on, my noble stallion,' she said to Simon Anderson. **'LET'S GO LICK THE TOENAILS OF ADVENTURE!'**

It was the third day of the festival and the final round of the Royal Turnip Tournament was about to begin.

seRious mud mounds↓

hay-bale hurdles →

The Tough Turnip Triathlon was a gruelling obstacle course which would see Queen McNiff and King Nutmeg take on three tricky challenges.

First, they'd race head-to-head in the Turnip and Spoon Race, negotiating a series of mud mounds and hay-bale hurdles.

Then, they'd wade through the Muddy Bog of Muckiness, collecting as many turnips as they could grab.

Finally – the moment for which every serious athlete tirelessly trains – they would Bake Some Cakes. With the remaining time on the clock (and their freshly plucked turnips), the competitors would each make a traditional turnip cake. These

BAKE OFF!

muddy
bog of
muckiness

delicious creations would then be judged by world-renowned chef, Horatio Whisk (inventor of the birthday cake).

At the Green Arena, the crowd were already cheering, **'PREHEAT, PREHEAT, PREHEAT'** to remind the contestants to turn their ovens on early. But little did they know that trouble was brewing. Beverly had made her way to the Green Arena to inform the queen about the missing orb.

'Your pal's been a very naughty goose,' Beverly told King Nutmeg and the Wobby Rock gang, who were sitting with Queen McNiff. 'She broke into the queen's vault last night.'

'She wouldn't do that!' said Elle Emen-O'Pea.

'Yes, she would, and she did. The silly goose is on the loose with the Orb of Ogg!'

Plumm tutted. 'I'm afraid your friend has fluffed up, big time.'

'Misty Jamjar must have tricked Betty into it!' said Figg. 'Queen McNiff, you know that sprite can't

142

be trusted.'

'That's enough!' Queen McNiff held up her eyebrows to silence the group. 'I'm not going to let this spoil the final day of the Turnip Festival. We'll send out a search party. But in the meantime, Beverly will keep watch here, while Nutters and I finish the Royal Turnip Tournament.'

Everyone agreed, because Queen McNiff was so strict and important and because she threatened to give them all detention if they said another word.

The final round of the Royal Turnip Tournament was the decider. Would Queen McNiff or King Nutmeg win the coveted Turnip Cup?

OK, reader, I want you to imagine you're in the front row of the Green Arena. You're sitting next to Pam and Pamm, with a shoe full of popcorn and a heart full of happiness. Suddenly, Plumm blows one of those curly party whistles to signal the start of the race. The hair on the back of your neck stands up and yells, **'VEGETABLES!'**

You watch in awe as the two monarchs hastily
start the course, each balancing a proud turnip
on their spoon. They clear the first hay bale with
magnificent leaps. They sprint over the first mound
like agile ostriches. As they round the corner,
they're neck and neck. But suddenly, King Nutmeg
drops his turnip. 'Blast my beard with a banjo!' he
cries.

'Turnip down!' cries Rupert Sometimes from the
audience.

144

'Keep going!' shouts Elle Emen-O'Pea.

The king takes his battered turnip back to the start line and begins the course again. This is going to cost him. He's less steady on his feet this time, the stress turning his limbs to porridge. But he speeds through the obstacles as best he can, keeping his cheeky vegetable firmly on the spoon.

As the king reaches the Muddy Bog of Muckiness, Queen McNiff has already waded halfway through the gloopy swamp, her arms full of plump turnips. The only veggies that are left now are the tiddly ones and the wonky ones. The turnips that sigh and weep, 'Nobody loves us.'

But King Nutmeg embraces those sad little vegetables. 'You're coming with me,' he says, commando-crawling through the sludge. On and on he scrambles. Ahead, he spies the queen already peeling her turnips in the kitchen. Time is slipping away.

His arms shake. His bones creak. His skin glows

145

(mud is very good for the pores). **'UGH,'** he shouts. **'I CAN'T DO THIS!'**

'HURRY UP, DADDY!' shout Pam and Pamm. **'WE NEED A WEE!'**

Their loyal cries give King Nutmeg one last boost of energy. He heaves himself through the mud like a heroic hippo. Dripping with muck, he slops to the kitchen and drops his meagre collection of turnips on the counter. As he catches his breath, Queen McNiff has already got her spoon in a mixing bowl, stirring herself silly.

Figg sidles up to King Nutmeg. 'Get baking, Your Majesty.'

'How can I?' the king groans, wiping the dirt from his hands. 'I don't have enough turnips to fill a cake tin.'

Figg checks his **BOOGER,** his heart hammering. Now's the time to make it up to the king, once and for all. He has to advise like he's never advised before. 'How about a little cupcake?'

146

'No, no. I couldn't possibly make a cupcake. They're so **SMALL**,' wails the king.

'Small but mighty,' says Figg.

'Small but . . . *mighty*?' Realisation smacks King Nutmeg in the face like a lost pigeon. 'Oh, Figg, I've been an absolute jam sandwich. Little cupcakes are amazing! They're powerful and zesty and full of punch. Just like our Betty!' He shakes his head as he starts chopping his turnips. 'I've been such a fool.'

Figg smiles. **YIPPEE!** That was some darn good advising he just did. He can finally forgive himself. He can look his laminator in the face once more. **TASTY REDEMPTION!**

'By broccoli, I should be proud to show Betty off!' cries the king. 'She's the best little cupcake in the world! A miniscule miracle. A pint-sized pro. Oh, if only I could apologise to her right now.'

Reader, just imagine, as you're sitting there with a mouth full of popcorn, that the ground

suddenly begins to shake. **BOOM! BIFF!**
BADONK! Something's coming. Something
big.

An enormous crop of curls rises on the horizon.

A shadow creeps over the arena.

King Nutmeg gulps.

Is it a tree? A monster? **A HUGE,**
ANGRY GERBIL?!

Come on, reader, don't be ridiculous.
IT'S BIG BETTY.

BEES IN SPACE

Bees in space! Bees in space!
Interstellar insect fun
Bees in space! Bees in space!
Astrobuzzin' round the sun

Bees in space! Bees in space!
Honeycomb hyperdrive
Bees in space! Bees in space!
Zero gravity hive

Tiny little space suits (Bees in space!)
Three pairs of moon boots (Bees in space!)
Planet pollination (Bees in space!)
Goin' on vacation to the BEE SPACE STATION!

Bees in space! Bees in space!
Wait! Is that a black hole?
Bees in space! Bees in space!
Better tell Mission Control

Come in, Mission Control...

This is Mission Control. Are you there, bees?
Bees? Oh dear. I do hope they didn't get sucked
into that black hole!
I guess we should have considered that possibility
when we sent a swarm of bees to space.
Oh well. Onwards and upwards.

by Clammy Pete

Yikes. I wasn't expecting that dark turn at the end.

he crowd went **BLUEBERRIES** at the sight of big Betty (which, if you didn't know, means they threw their arms up and screamed with pure terror).

Queen McNiff dropped her pudding bowl. 'We're under attack!'

'Code Cucumber!' said Plumm, instructing the guards to fight back.

'I'M NOT A BADDIE!' bellowed Betty,

peering into the arena as though she was staring down a toilet bowl. **'I'M THE GUARDIAN OF UPPER CRUST AND I'M HERE TO SAVE YOU!'**

'TWADDLE CAKES!' shouted the audience in perfect unison. **'WE DON'T BELIEVE YOU!'**

But the Crossword Crew believed her! They were loyal as lollipops.

'Let's go!' said Rupert Sometimes, as Figg and Elle Emen-O'Pea clambered on to his back. Just as they were flying up to Betty, however, the sound of huge, fluttering wings made the air vibrate.

Was it a dragon? An alien? **A CONFUSED SEAGULL IN A PUFFER JACKET?!**

Come on, reader, don't be absurd. It was Misty Jamjar. **AND SHE WAS GIGANTIC.**

'MISTY?' cried the queen.

'YOU THINK I'D LET YOU GET AWAY WITH FIRING ME?' The sprite flicked back her pink hair, causing a huge gust of wind.

'YOU RUINED MY FUN, SO NOW I'M GOING TO RUIN YOURS.' She looked down at the Orb of Ogg, which she was wearing as a necklace. 'THIS THING IS CRAZY BEANS, BY THE WAY!'

Betty scowled. 'JAMJAR, GIVE THAT ORB BACK!'

Misty rolled her huge eyes. 'OH, IT'S YOU. YOU THINK YOU'RE SO TOUGH, BUT YOU'LL NEVER BEAT ME NOW I HAVE ALL THIS POWER.'

Misty was very pleased with herself because she had created a mega army with the Orb's magic. An elite band of baddies designed to bring maximum disruption to the Turnip Festival.

She snapped her fingers. **DING!**

A gang of humongous sprites, carrying water pistols, began circling overhead like hungry vultures.

She snapped them again. **DANG!**

154

Three massive trolls came stomping into the
arena with wooden thumpin' sticks and T-shirts that
said: **TURNIPS ARE GROSS.**

Then she snapped her fingers once more.
DONG!

155

The infamous Gruff Goats emerged from the nearby trees looking really cheesed off and ready to fight. Misty had powered them up with some serious and incredibly dangerous magic. Now they could shoot cotton wool out of their earholes! No, hang on. That's not quite right. What was it again? Oh, that's it. They could shoot lasers from their eyeballs!

Then Misty did something extra sneaky. She held the Orb and cried, **'SPARKLE TIME.'**

In a puff of smoke, a gigantic bottle of sparkly nail varnish appeared.

Queen McNiff's face dropped. **'DON'T DO IT, MISTY!'**

Plumm gasped. **'NO, NO. REMEMBER THE RULES!'**

Misty unscrewed the lid and tipped the gloopy polish into the centre of the arena. **'WHOOPS!'** she cried, with a naughty guffaw.

'STOP!' cried the queen, in a sea of sparkles.

'GLITTERY NAIL VARNISH ISN'T APPROPRIATE!'

Betty saw something zooming towards her face. She flinched and got ready to strike before realising it was her old pals, the Crossword Crew.

'Betty!' cried Elle Emen-O'Pea.

'Oh, my friends!' said Betty. 'I'm so . . .' The words caught in her throat. 'So . . .' She took a deep breath. 'One across. Five letters. An expression of regret.'

Figg understood. 'Me too,' he said.

'Me three,' said Elle Emen-O'Pea.

Rupert Sometimes looked up at his pal and smiled. 'Me four.'

Betty felt her heart ache. **I'M SO SORRY,'** she said, with a tear the size of a roast chicken running down her cheek.

Yay! The Crossword Crew were reunited once again, **THE UTTER LEGENDS.**

'Right, enough of this lovey-dovey stuff,' said

157

Betty. 'I've got to get **BATTLE READY!'**

Betty summoned the strength of the trees, the power of the wind and the confidence of a really cool person in leather trousers. Then she checked her pockets. 'Where is it? Where is it?!'

Simon Anderson neighed and nudged the can of Bad Gas towards her.

'Thanks, Simon Anderson! Hmmm. I was hoping my can of scrumptious scent had magically grown too. Oh well.' Betty pinched the little can between her thumb and finger and, aiming at her huge, cavernous armpits, sprayed a few tiny puffs.

Luckily, a few puffs of Bad Gas was all she needed. Betty found herself at **ONE HUNDRED AND FOUR PER CENT** power and ready to clonk Misty on the noggin.

Looming over the arena like two huge monsters, Betty and Misty began to grapple with each other.

MONSTERS?! Oh, golly gherkins, reader, this is getting a bit scary for me now. I think I might go and hide behind a pillow. Let me know when it's over.

Awkward pause

Ah. That's embarrassing. I just remembered that I'm the author and nothing is going to happen if I don't write it. I suppose I should stop cuddling my special little blankie and pick up my pen.

Back to the brutal and harrowing battle.

So, Betty and Misty looked at each other and said, 'Make friends, make friends, never, never break friends!' Then they went to the bowling alley and had a brilliant time and drank slushies and won loads of money on the 2p coin pusher.

Sorry, reader. I've just received another letter.

Dear Salvador Catflap,

Come on! We all know that isn't what really happened, you scaredy, scaredy Nappy-Bum Baby!

Fess up,

Dave Schoolboy

HOW DARE HE CALL ME A LIAR?

I'll have you know that Betty and Misty were instant besties and won loads of teddies on the grabber machine.

Oh, who am I kidding? No one ever wins on the grabber machine. Fine. That wasn't what happened at all. Betty and Misty weren't BFFs. They were WEEs (Worst Enemies Eternally). And they were brawling outside the Green Arena like a couple of raging raccoons.

Misty held the Orb and conjured a giant spear that shot out purple electric sparks. Betty looked around for a weapon to match its power, setting her sights on a long, pointy turnip. But when she held it up, it looked pathetic.

Misty laughed. **'YOU'RE TOAST, STEADY!'**

Reconsidering her choice of weapon, Betty snapped a long flagpole from the top of the arena. **'YEAH?'** she said, wielding the flag. **'WELL, YOU'RE FLAGHETTI BOLOGNAISE!'**

'**YAY, FLAGS RULE!**' said Johnny Logflume, nearly peeing his pants with excitement.

They clonked weapons. **ZAP!** Betty felt a surge of electricity through her long limbs. But she pushed through the fizzy feeling and fought on with determination and static hair.

THWACK! Betty prodded the sprite's arm with the flagpole.

Misty winced, then aimed her sizzling spear at Betty's shoulder. As Betty backflipped out of the way, Simon Anderson clung on for dear life. Betty landed with a huge thud, sending a tremor through Upper Crust. She recovered quickly and swung her flag at Misty, skimming the top of her wings.

Giant Betty gave Misty a series of impressive clobbers, cartwheeling like a supercharged Ferris wheel. The sprite fought back and gave Betty a run of nasty shocks. The two massive rivals loomed above the awestruck crowd as Betty thwacked Misty's hand and snapped off a nail.

'HEY!' said Misty, flying out of reach as she nursed her finger. **'YOU'VE GONE TOO FAR NOW.'**

'GET BACK DOWN HERE!'

Betty tried to grab Misty, but the sprite flew even higher. Misty then took the Orb from her necklace and placed it on top of the spear. It grew and glowed with energy, creating an All-Powerful

Weapon of Nastiness.

'**HAHAHA!**' said Misty, shooting purple lightning bolts.

Above them, the over-sized sprite gang were circling the arena, spraying the innocent citizens with tepid water. The crowd roared with screams of '**HELP!**', '**I'M SO WET!**' and '**IT WOULDN'T BE SO BAD IF THE WATER WAS A BIT WARMER!**'

Rupert Sometimes gulped. 'Blimey! If Misty shoots those lightning bolts anywhere near all this water and nail varnish, she'll electrocute the whole arena!'

So like a brave little sausage roll, the gentleman owl soared up towards the water-wielding, super-soaking sprites. On his back, Figg used his rolled-up **BOOGER** to swat their feet, and Elle Emen-O'Pea bashed their behinds with the pointy end of her trumpet.

Misty shot a series of nasty electric sparks at the crowd, while the three dopey trolls got busy

163

clonkin' with their thumpin' sticks.
(Their terrible aim was outweighed by
their meaty strength.)

Betty peered up at Misty Jamjar and
her evil electric sparks. Treading on
a window ledge to get a leg-up, she
made a daring leap. **'ONE, TWO,
THREE, FOUR, FIVE,'** she said, grabbing
Misty by the ankle. **'ONCE I CAUGHT A
FISH ALIVE!'**

Misty struggled to get away.

'It's no use,' cried Betty. 'Linda and Gregg are
bigger and stronger than ever!'

But the sprite grinned like an otter in a race car.
'Not for long!' And she waved the Orb and zapped

Betty with a huge bolt of lightning.

Betty felt her body deflating like a broken bouncy castle. Suspended mid-air in a forcefield of purple energy, she withered and wrinkled. Simon Anderson tumbled from her shoulder and floated majestically beside her. In a sudden blast of bright light, Betty was shrunk to her regular human height. The size she was before the Toad Witch's evil spell. (Shrinking! Growing! Honestly, I can't keep track.)

Misty pulled a fake frown. **'NOT SO STRONG ANY MORE? SHAME.'** She snapped her fingers and the forcefield disappeared, leaving Betty and Simon Anderson to plummet to the ground.

Chapter 14

ow, where were we? Oh yes, the big, exciting climax of our story.

So Betty and Simon Anderson were at the school disco, playing musical bumps . . . No, wait. That's not right. They were at the soft play, holding hands down the big slide . . . Hang on, that's not right either.

What were they doing again? Oh, that's it. They were plummeting to their death.

'**NOOOOO!**' cried Betty, as she tumbled into the

Green Arena, human-sized once more.

'   !' said Simon Anderson, because he couldn't talk.

Betty knew she had to act fast, or she and her trusty horse would be splat sauce. As she hurtled towards the ground, she looked around hopefully.

Falling alongside her was the flagpole she'd been using as a weapon. In a flash, she reached across and ripped the flag from the pole, then held it up high and gripped the corners to make a parachute. Slowing, she pulled the flag down hard on one side and manoeuvred herself on to Simon Anderson's saddle, her rear end fitting perfectly like the old days. Together, the pair floated down like a couple of delicate goose feathers, landing in the middle of the arena to great applause.

Johnny Logflume nearly fainted at the sight of such exquisite flagwork.

'FNARPH!' said the audience in perfect unison, just as a load of awesome battle stuff

167

began to happen all around them. **THAT WAS SERIOUSLY COOL!'**

I suggest you imagine this next bit set to some really dramatic music. Something like *Wheels on the Bus*. The Green Arena descended into madness, the tepid water and nail varnish whipping everyone into a frenzy. (Actually, on second thoughts, perhaps *Wheels on the Bus* doesn't quite work. Maybe try something like *Dreadful Sound of Doom in G Minor*.)

Anyway, the Gruff Goats managed to scale the arena wall and began blasting unsuspecting crowd members with lasers from their eyeballs. Meanwhile, Beverly and the other Upper Crust guards began shooting flaming arrows at the sprites, and the Crossword Crew whizzed around the trio of trolls, trying to make them dizzy.

On the other side of the stadium, Sir Loin of Beef and Johnny Logflume protected King Nutmeg with the age-old alliance of sword and soggy flag, as Queen McNiff armed herself with a wooden baking spoon.

After some nasty laser-shooting, the goats commenced their ambush. I'm sure you remember the drill, but just in case you need a reminder, they started by lobbing a load of potatoes into the crowd, then they bellyflopped into the arena for some hand-to-horn combat. (All except Gilbert, who was too scared to jump from such a height and cowered on the high wall, sucking his hoof.)

169

'Take that!' said the queen, clonking a goat with her spoon.

'You lot can jolly well jog on!' said Sir Loin of Beef, chasing a group of goats away with his sword held high. (His bad back ached a little but his wolf tattoo spurred him on like a loyal old friend.)

'FLAGHETTI CARBONARA!' said Johnny Logflume, poking a goat with his flagpole and completely ripping off Betty's new catchphrase. Unfortunately, he didn't say it with much oomph, so the goat wasn't the least bit intimidated.

However, in a twist no one saw coming, Johnny Logflume suddenly remembered he could do kung fu! **'OMG**, I totally forgot I could do kung fu!' he said, as he roundhouse-kicked the goat into next week. 'What am I like, eh?! I'd forget my head if it wasn't screwed on!' Then he hook-punched twelve goats in quick succession, leaving them groaning in a pile on the floor.

Rupert Sometimes darted about the arena like

a zippy little rocket, while Figg and Elle Emen-O'Pea held tight. The flying owl confused the trolls so much that the largest and smelliest one accidentally biffed the other two on the head, before walking head first into the sign for the toilets.

'Got him!' said Rupert Sometimes, as the troll landed with a heavy bang.

'Ugh,' moaned Misty Jamjar, realising the good guys were fighting back like pros. She aimed her All-Powerful Weapon of Nastiness at Gilbert the goat and grumbled, 'I suppose I'm going to have to create an All-Powerful Goat of Grumpiness now!'

In a flash of light, Gilbert grew into a massive monster-goat and began stomping on terrified Upper Crusters.

'Misty Jamjar!' said Queen McNiff in a very firm voice, her eyebrows coming together in an angry tango. 'Put that orb down this instant. Your disagreement is with me, not these innocent people. Let's have a reasonable conversation.'

Misty yawned. 'I'd rather cause a load of destruction, thanks, Queenie.'

Alas, her nasty plan was working. The Green Arena was a picture of carnage. Fire. Flood. Fabulous nail polish. Creatures of all shapes and sizes giving each other a proper good walloping.

Betty rode Simon Anderson towards King Nutmeg, who was cowering next to his turnips in the kitchen.

'Oh, Betty!' the king whimpered. 'I'm so glad you're here to protect us!'

'Really?' Betty said. 'Me?' Though there was turmoil all around, she felt a glimmer of hope in her full-sized heart.

'Betty Steady, you're the **BEST WARRIOR I'VE EVER KNOWN!'** said the king, rising to his feet. 'I was a right nitwit, thinking you were too little. My royal apologies.'

Betty and the king stood before each other,

172

almost the same height for once, ready for a heart-to-heart. But at that very moment, Gilbert the All-Powerful Goat of Grumpiness shot a massive laser beam their way.

'DUCK!' said Betty.

(Reader, I hope you didn't think I was going to make a duck joke there. What do you take me for?)

Anyway, King Nutmeg bent down just in time as a ~~duck~~ *laser* flew over him.

'Worry not,' said Betty, searching her satchel for a

rope, brave as a bread bin. 'I'll take that goat down!'

Like a cool cowgirl, she spun her rope into a huge lasso and threw it over one of the goat's horns. As she pulled down, Gilbert fell to his hairy knees.

'Well done, Linda and Gregg!' Betty cried, straining with all her human-sized might. 'You're still winners!'

Misty had been watching from above. 'Oh, stop being so annoying!' She screwed up her nose in frustration and pointed her spear at Betty. 'Right. You can be a tiddly little pipsqueak again.'

Betty was hit by another blast. Everything went all wibbly-wobbly. And in a haze of zingy electric magic, she felt herself shrinking. **'OH, HEAVENLY HANDS OF FATE!'** she said, landing with a pint-sized plop on Simon Anderson's saddle. 'I'm back to the size of a jar of pickled onions!'

Gilbert breathed a massive sigh of relief. 'That squirt doesn't stand a chance!'

174

Sure, tiny Betty was ridiculously undersized. But King Nutmeg knew she would protect them with every ounce of her teeny-weeny soul. 'Betty,' he said. 'Just remember . . . you're small but you can brawl!'

By broccoli, he was right!

Feeling a surge of confidence, Betty grabbed the rope and yanked. It was like a tree trunk in her tiny hands, but she clung on tight. Linda and Gregg bulged and flexed like there was no tomorrow, pulling the All-Powerful Goat of Grumpiness to the ground.

'Blimey, that squirt has some muscles on her!' said the big bleater, as Sir Loin of Beef and Johnny Logflume tied him up so he couldn't budge.

'Quick,' Betty said to the king. She gazed up at the enormous Misty, who was wielding her weapon like a baddie with a nasty next move. 'I need all your turnips.'

As the king handed over his turnip stash, Betty

fashioned a makeshift catapult from some kitchen tongs and Simon Anderson's tiger-print cycling shorts. (Believe me, that stallion gasped as she unexpectedly whipped them off.) She loaded a turnip in the stretchy fabric, pulled it back and pinged it up towards the sprite.

The faithful vegetable hit Misty on the leg. **'HEY, STOP THAT!'** she said. But Betty shot another turnip, this time biffing the mega-sprite right in the belly button.

'Excellent, Betty!' cried the queen, making a mental note to award her with an Effie the Effort Elephant badge. 'A commendable shot.'

Misty'd had quite enough of bothersome Betty and the queen. So she flew down to the arena and picked Queen McNiff up. Squashed between the sprite's glittery fingernails, the queen flinched at such a show of sparkling disobedience.

Beverly strode across the arena, her hairdo swinging with rage. With a grunt, she swung Choppy

Bob at the giant sprite's feet. **'PUT HER DOWN!'**

Misty flicked Beverly away with her shoe just as another turnip struck her from behind. She spun around to look for Betty. 'Where are you, little crossword nerd? Come on. Show your face!'

Another turnip came at her from the direction of the kitchen. Misty put the queen down and stuck her All-Powerful Weapon of Nastiness in the ground.

'Guard that!' she said to the few undefeated goats. Then she got down on her hands and knees for a better look, coming face to face with King Nutmeg holding a muffin tin.

'What you got there?' said Misty suspiciously.

'Just . . . just a little cupcake,' the king stammered.

The sprite narrowed her eyes at the baking tin. The holes were all empty except one, which held a single cupcake topped with curly auburn frosting. The king gulped.

'Eww,' massive Misty said. 'Turnip cakes are gross.' Then she turned away in search of Betty.

At that moment, the little cupcake burst out of the tin. It wasn't a cake at all! It was teeny-tiny Betty! She grabbed her catapult and launched a turnip as hard as she could. It whizzed past Misty Jamjar's head.

The sprite tossed back her hair and chuckled. 'You missed!'

Betty grinned and flicked back her own hair. 'No, I didn't.'

Misty's smile dropped as she followed Betty's gaze and saw the turnip hit the All-Powerful Weapon of Nastiness. With a crack, the Orb snapped off and spun into the air.

Mini Betty gave herself a fist pump. **'THREE BLIND MICE!'**

Misty's huge eyes widened. **'CATCH IT!'** she shouted to the gormless goats.

As the goats reached up with their hairy legs, the Orb of Ogg tumbled down. The arena fell silent. Betty's heart raced. Simon Anderson realised his bottom was completely on display without his shorts on. But just as the bleaty bandits nearly had their hooves on the glowing orb . . . a mystery figure swooped down from the sky and nabbed it!

The crowd gasped. Who was this brave rider? This soaring star? This airborne hero of the sky?

Well, waddaya know? It was a fine old owl, with

an imp and a mouse on his back.

Betty beamed with pride as her beloved friends carried the Orb to safety like a trio of utter champs. **'YEAH!'** she cried. **'CROSSWORD CREW!'**

MELVIN

Melvin the bee couldn't make honey, no matter
how hard he tried.
He did the usual method (pouring in the nectar
and waving his hands around).
But instead of delicious yellow honey, it always
came out as something unexpected.
Like a bookmark. Or a friendship bracelet.
He just couldn't see where he was going wrong.
One day, he asked the queen bee for advice.
She looked at him with her five passionate eyes and said,
'Melvin, I'm very busy. You'll have to come
back another time.'

By Clammy Pete

I think he's lost it.

 limey. That ending was all a bit tense, wasn't it?

You'll be glad to know that good old Queen McNiff used the Orb of Ogg to turn Misty Jamjar and her sneaky sidekicks back to their normal selves.

'Wait, I was only joking!' said the sprite, flapping her tiny wings as Beverly dragged her away for an extra-long detention. 'Ugh. You people need to lighten up!' The crowd booed her as she left.

The Green Arena was in chaos. Sorry, I meant Chaos was in the Green Arena. With her pixie pal, Mayhem. They'd seen the whole thing and were quite frankly worn out and couldn't wait to get home and do some knitting with a cup of hot cocoa. Anyway, the Green Arena was a right mess. The audience were in shock and soaking wet, but they were thrilled that the baddies had been put in their place.

Smiling, the queen shook Betty's little hand. 'That was some A-star fighting!'

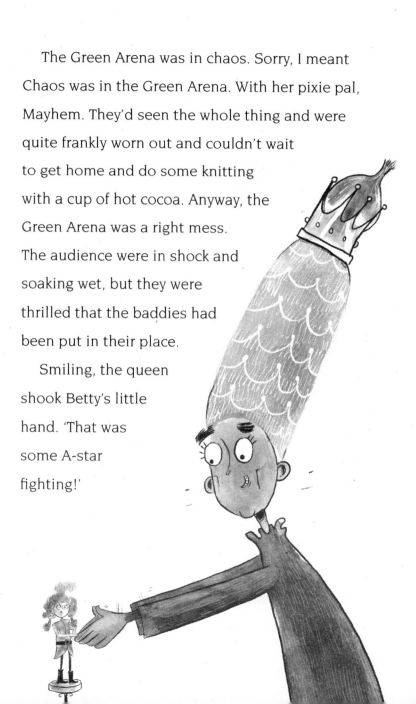

'Oh, Your Majesty,' said Betty. 'Beverly was right. I'm such a silly goose. I should never have taken the Orb.'

'True,' said the queen. 'You made a bad choice. But you learned from your mistake.' She held up the Orb and wiped away a smudge. 'That's better. Now, Betty, I have a proposition for you. With the power of the Orb, I could make you any size you like.'

'I could be tall again?!' Betty felt exhausted. Tall. Tiny. Bloomin' massive. She couldn't keep up with all this. And yet, this was what she'd wanted, wasn't it? A chance to be her old legendary self again.

'I could make you tall, yes,' said the queen. 'But . . .'

Betty held her breath. There was always a big, juicy **BUT.**

The queen let her eyebrows soften like hairy butter. 'But you'd need to stay here in Upper Crust.'

'Here?' asked Betty. 'Why?'

'The Orb's magic is only temporary,' said the

queen. 'To keep you at full height, I'd need to re-cast the spell regularly. Luckily, we could use a top-notch guard like you around here.'

'Golly gherkins!' said King Nutmeg, with a gulp. 'The thought of losing you, Betty!' He stroked his beard and reminded himself that she was never his little pet. 'But . . . I would understand if you chose to stay here with Niffy. I've not given you the stinking respect you deserve.'

Elle Emen-O'Pea took Betty's hand. 'You should do what makes you happy, Betty.'

Betty's bunch of loyal chums stared at her in anticipation. Could they really be about to lose the great Guardian of Wobbly Rock?

'WIND THE BOBBIN UP!' said Betty, slapping her thigh. 'I don't even need to think about it! Queen McNiff, your kingdom is wonderful. But my home is Wobbly Rock!'

'Well, clonk my crown with a clarinet!' said King Nutmeg.

'Hooray for tiny Betty!' said Pam and Pamm, before starting a chant of '**BOOGLE-OOGLE-BLIM-BLAM!**'

What a celebration! Elle Emen-O'Pea played a jazzy version of *Wheels on the Bus* while Figg and Rupert Sometimes danced a happy waltz. The Queen gave Betty an Effie the Effort Elephant badge and a firm handshake. Everyone was merry as marshmallows. Well, everyone except Plumm, who was looking down at her clipboard and frowning.

'There's going to be a lot of paperwork,' said the queen's imp.

'Paperwork?!' said Figg, feeling like his perfect organised self again. 'I can help you with that!'

'The Green Arena cleaners are going to have quite a job on their hands!' said Plumm. 'Where are they, anyway? I'm sure they were here yesterday.'

Betty kept very quiet.

'Right,' said the queen, addressing the audience.

'You can all leave in single file.'

'Wait!' Figg shouted. 'We've not even concluded the Royal Turnip Tournament! No one finished making their cakes!'

'Oh, don't you worry about that!' said an extremely smooth and calming voice. Everyone turned around to see a lovely man in a chef's hat.

Rupert Sometimes gasped. 'It's Horatio Whisk. Inventor of the birthday cake!'

'Yes,' said the lovely man. 'It's me. Horatio Whisk. Inventor of the birthday cake!'

'It's really you!' said Plumm, astounded by his sheer loveliness. 'Blast! We don't have anything for you to judge.'

Horatio Whisk gave a smile like a thousand sunsets. 'No problem, sweet imp. I saw everything! And I'm so proud of each and every one of you for being such good eggs!'

'Ooh! He's proud of us!' said King Nutmeg, beaming with joy.

'So,' said Horatio Whisk, unveiling a turnip-shaped trophy. 'The winner of the Royal Turnip Tournament is . . .' He paused as King Nutmeg and Queen McNiff linked arms and shared excited looks. 'Sir Loin of Beef!'

'Huh?' said King Nutmeg.

Sir Loin stepped forward sheepishly, holding a Turnip Battenberg. 'Oh, yes. Sorry. I whipped this cake up while you lot were chatting.'

'Actually, on second thoughts,' said Horatio Whisk, 'you're all winners!'

'YAAAY!' said Niffy and Nutters, raising the trophy to the sky.

'Birthday cake for everyone!' said Horatio Whisk,

wheeling out a trolley of delicious puddings.

'WOO-HOO!' cried Betty. 'And it's not even anyone's birthday!'

'Actually,' said a quiet voice, 'it's *my* birthday.'

'Wait. Who said that?' asked Betty.

Andy Underarm, the queen's messenger, emerged from the crowd.

'Has he been here the whole time?' whispered King Nutmeg.

Queen McNiff shrugged.

'Well, happy birthday, young chap!' said Horatio Whisk, giving him a big hug. 'Have some cake!'

'I'd rather have a fizzy pop!' Andy Underarm said. 'I've been waiting ages for it, and I'm getting *pretty* thirsty.'

'On a school night? I don't think so,' said Queen McNiff. Then she held up the Orb of Ogg and smiled. 'Only joking! Bottomless fizzy pop all round!' As she spoke, a magical fountain of soda appeared.

'Best birthday ever!' said Andy Underarm, grabbing a cup of bubbly delight. And, just as he took a sip, feeling as though life was truly magical, he thought he caught sight of Nanny Turnip soaring overhead on her flying alligator.

Oh, what an enchanting end to the Turnip Festival! The Upper Crusters and the Wobbly Rockers partied all night long. Simon Anderson left his

shorts off because he was feeling cheeky. Figg and Rupert Sometimes set up a massive crossword for everyone, and Elle Emen-O'Pea played a special rendition of *Fish Finger Boogie* (*the Remix*). And Betty and Johnny Logflume spent half the evening making up such hilarious flag puns that they kept squirting fizzy pop out of their noses. What a night!

Hang on, reader. Another letter's arrived.

Dear Salvador Catflap,

Horatio Whisk? Andy Underarm? Nanny Turnip riding a flying alligator!? These people have nothing to do with the story. This is absolutely ridiculous. But for some reason... I LOVE IT!

What a thrilling tale! I forgive you for being a complete nincompoop. Please write another Betty book soon because there's literally nothing more exciting. Not even cheese on toast.

Yours joyfully,

Dave Schoolboy

Oh, reader! What a ride we've had.

Thanks so much for coming on this adventure. You've been such a good little cherub. I do hope we'll see each other again soon for some more Wobbly Rock fun. But for now, there's just time for a final word from Betty . . .

'**FNARPH!**' said Betty.

And here's one last poem from our pal Clammy Pete to send us on our way. I wonder what nonsense he's got in store for us this time? Don't forget to give him some feedback. There's a handy form for you to fill in on the next page. Until next time, old friend.

AWKWARD SERIOUS POEM

Look, I know I'm a bit of a crackpot, but bees
really are superb little fellas.
They pollinate plants and crops like absolute heroes.
Unfortunately, because humans have fluffed up the
planet, bees are dying out.
Bigwigs with big powers need to change things.
But there are things we can do too.
Like planting wildflowers and creating cool bee
discos in our gardens.
So, if you're interested, why not read up about
how to help?
And next time you see a bee, don't forget to tell them that
Clammy Pete loves them very much.

By Clammy Pete

Poetry Feedback by _____

I think Clammy Pete's poems are: (please tick)

Absolute twaddle cakes

Bonkers but brill

A little too focused on bees

Favourite poem

_____

Least favourite poem

_____

If you could compare Clammy Pete to a packet of crisps, what flavour would he be and why? _____

_____

_____

How many times did you shout, 'OH, BEES, YOU'RE SO GORGEOUS!' when reading these poems?

7

29

432

Never, obviously

Favourite line of poetry _____

_____

Favourite line of symmetry (please draw) _____

_____

Do you like honey?

Yes

No

Tractors

General comments _____

_____

Draw a picture of a lovely bee

THANKS FOR YOUR FEEDBACK!

Don't miss the first Betty Steady adventure,
or Linda and Gregg will duff you up!

Coming soon . . .
Iced bun, JOB DONE!

Nicky Smith-Dale

Nicky spent her childhood in daydreams, floating through life in a haze of stories and silliness. When she grew up (and had to impersonate a sensible adult) she tried a few uninspiring career options before discovering that teaching was a lot of fun. Then she decided to write some silly stories about a hero called Betty Steady. It was weird but it worked I guess?

Sarah Horne

Sarah Horne learned to draw while trying to explain her reasoning for an elaborate haircut at the age of nine. She has illustrated over 100 books and started her career illustrating for newspapers. When not at her desk, Sarah loves running, painting, photography, cooking, film and a good stomp up a hill. She can mostly be found giggling under some paper in her London studio.